VENGEFUL VAMPIRE AT WONKY INN

WONKY INN BOOK 8

JEANNIE WYCHERLEY

Vengeful Vampire at Wonky Inn
Wonky Inn Book 8
by

JEANNIE WYCHERLEY

Copyright © 2019 Jeannie Wycherley
Bark at the Moon Books
All rights reserved

Publishers note: This is a work of fiction. All characters, names, places and incidents are either products of the author's imagination or are used fictitiously and for effect or are used with permission. Any other resemblance to actual persons, either living or dead, is entirely coincidental.

No part of this book may be reproduced, distributed or transmitted in any form or by any means, including photocopying, recording, or other electronic or mechanical methods, or by any information storage and retrieval system without the prior written permission of the publisher, except in the case of very brief quotations embodied in critical reviews and certain other non-commercial uses permitted by copyright law.

Sign up for Jeannie's newsletter:
eepurl.com/cN3Q6L

Vengeful Vampire at Wonky Inn was edited by Anna Bloom @ The Indie Hub

Cover design by JC Clarke of The Graphics Shed.
Formatting by Tammy

CHAPTER ONE

"*Parva venire magicis viventem!*" A bolt of blue light shot out from the tip of my wand.

Something intent on a quick escape—and to be honest it could just have been a large purple squirrel—scuttled away at high speed making for the bushes. That wasn't the idea.

Beside me, Silvan tutted and levelled his own wand at the retreating creature. "*Evanescet.*"

The thing, whatever it might have been, evaporated into a wisp of steam.

"By all that's green, Alfhild," Silvan muttered in his most world-weary tone. "*What* is it that you are actually envisioning here?"

"I'm not sure." I giggled. "I'm tired." I flopped down onto my belly, ignoring the slightly damp feel of the grass beneath me. It was October after all.

"I've been up since half past five this morning. I'd quite like a nap."

"Go and have one, then." Silvan dropped to the ground beside me. "I would."

"You've only been up a few hours," I pointed out. "You don't need one."

"Naps are one of life's necessities. We should embrace every opportunity to nap whenever the occasion arises."

I shook my head at him. Like he needed any more sleep. He truly was an incorrigible rascal. "I daren't go to bed because I'd never wake up. Besides, I need to supervise afternoon tea. Florence has some guests coming."

"Florence has?" Silvan grinned in amusement.

I rolled over on to my back and chuckled along with him. "I know, I know. She's much in demand." Since Florence had been runner-up in a Witchflix baking show called *The Great Witchy Cake Off*, the world had been going mad for her. Behind us the grass was still recovering from the imprint of the giant marquee we'd had on the lawn while the programme had been filmed here in the grounds of my wonky inn. My once impeccable lawn had faded to a pale wan-looking yellow; we'd had little rain in the ten days since the production had wrapped. Over the past week I'd caught Ned, my loved-up general handyman ghost, out here most mornings and evenings surveying the damage and sucking the wind between his teeth. I didn't fret. It would all come right again. Soon the rains would arrive, the grass would be refreshed, and we would have our lustrous lawn once more.

"I'm getting so many emails addressed to Florence... and fan mail by the score. She gets more post than I do."

"And people are coming to see her?"

"Well she's invited a few people to tea. I don't see any harm in that."

"Are you charging them?" Silvan asked, ever the mercenary.

I reached over to thump his arm. "Of course I'm not charging them. What do you think I am? They're Florence's *guests*!"

Silvan caught my fist easily and immobilised it. You don't mess with a witch who is a master of the dark arts. His eyes glowed though as he held my hand captive, and a shiver stirred my insides. "You'll never be a millionaire," he scolded, but his tone was playful.

"I don't need to be a millionaire." I frowned at him. It worried me that all he seemed to care about was money at times. He lived his life as a witch for hire. He went wherever he'd been summoned by whoever agreed to pay him the highest reward.

"What do you want then, Alfhild?" he asked, his dark eyes soft on mine.

I shrugged. "What most people want. To be happy." It sounded trite and maybe it was, but in the eighteen months since inheriting the inn, I'd known amazing contentment. For sure there had been some crashing lows, but the good times outweighed the bad. I'd met people I would consider friends for life, such as my efficient hotel manager Charity, Millicent my nearest witchy neighbour, Vance the Ent who lived in Speckled Wood, and Mara, the emotional witch who lived in the back of beyond with her faery changeling, Harys. Then there was Finbarr and his annoying band of pixies. To be fair, I couldn't imagine life without any of them.

In addition, I'd worked with witches and wizards of sheer genius, such as Wizard Shadowmender, Mr Kephisto, and Penelope Quigwell. And of course I'd connected with deceased members of my family, namely my father Erik and great-grandmother Alfhild Gwynfyre Daemonne (or Gwyn as I called her), among other ghosts who would probably plague me forever in the afterlife too.

"You're obsessed with this inn." Silvan stretched out on his side and studied me from under a hooded gaze.

"I suppose I am." There could be no disputing the fact that I'd been charged with a great responsibility when I took it on. Initially I had no idea what it would come to mean. Now I understood implicitly that I acted only as the current custodian. I held it in trust for the generations that would come, and safeguarded the huge number of occupants, both inside the inn—my ghosts—and in the grounds and Speckled Wood beyond.

I met Silvan's gaze and held it. I didn't understand what, if anything, was happening between us, but he had to know that there could be no negotiation about my responsibility for Whittle Inn. I was here to stay.

He reached out a hand and it hovered in the air above my face. I thought he intended to cup my cheek and for a moment I wanted him to, but then, abruptly, he flicked something from the side of my forehead and the moment was gone.

"Spider," he explained, but the carefree way he said it didn't convince me.

"So what about you?" I asked, curious as to his ambitions for life.

He rolled onto his back and stared at the sky. My crazy imagination thought I saw an element of yearning in his expression, but when he noticed me scrutinising him, he pulled a face. "I'm going to make wads of cash and travel the world, live in a big house, drink a lot of whisky and carouse with dozens of women."

"Um hmm."

"I'll eschew all responsibility for anything and everything and everybody."

"Right," I said, my tone heavy with sarcasm. Is that really what he wanted? Well, as long as I knew. "Sounds like a plan."

I held my hand out above his face as he had done to me, my fingers gently massaging the air. Then I slapped his forehead—not particularly hard, just enough to make a noise—and shot to my feet as he reached for me to retaliate.

"Spider!" I shrieked and ran away, laughing fit to burst.

"What have you been up to?" Charity, my young inn manager, regarded me with amused suspicion as I raced into the kitchen. "Your cheeks are flushed."

"Are they?" I flapped my hands at my face to cool myself down. "I've been outside. Silvan's been teaching me how to conjure djinns."

"Djinns?"

"They're little creatures some witches and wizards use to do jobs for them. Like if you can't get into a certain space or something. Or if something is particularly dangerous, you can just conjure your djinn and tell them to do it."

Charity raised her eyebrows. She'd recently had one of them pierced. I was still getting used to the sight, but it kind of went with her current peroxide blonde ultra-short hairstyle. Unlike my wild self, Charity—while a little on the unconventional side—always managed to be immaculately turned out with flawless make-up and perfectly fresh clothes. I don't know how she did it. I was a dragged-through-a-hedge-backwards kind of girl. If I hadn't donned my witch's robes, you'd find me in a crumpled black t-shirt and a pair of ancient black jeans with my ridiculous hair scrunched up on top of my head for convenience.

"And you can do it now, can you? Conjure a djinn?"

"No," I admitted. "Mine keep running off." In fact without Silvan's intervention, there would have been a dozen or more roaming the Whittlecombe countryside and wreaking havoc.

"Hmm." Charity didn't sound surprised. "And does conjuring these things involve rolling around on the damp grass?" She eyed me with scepticism, and I glanced guiltily down at my now green-tinged grey robes.

"I've been having a rest." I arched my own eyebrows at her, feigning innocence.

She nodded, a knowing look on her face. "Well listen, oh-magnificent-djinn-conjuring-boss-of-mine," she said. "Florence's guests are due here any minute. I really don't think they need to see you looking like that."

"Where is Florence?" I asked. The kitchen smelled of freshly baked scones, and cinnamon swirls. Pretty serving platters of freshly made sandwiches— delicate triangles of egg and cress, ham and tomato, salmon and cucumber—had been laid out on one of the work surfaces, ready to be carried through to the bar, along with small ramekins containing freshly made blackberry jam and enormous bowls of clotted cream.

My mouth watered.

"Laying the tables in the bar."

"*Tables?*" I queried. "How many tables?" Come

to think of it, there was an awful lot of food for a couple of guests. "How many people are we expecting?"

"*Florence* is expecting eight people. *We're* staying out of it," Charity reminded me. "This is her affair. Remember?"

I sighed in slight exasperation. I was happy for Florence. Of course I was. But I wanted a cream scone too. "Alright."

"I sense your reluctance." Charity smirked. "I think you need a little job to keep you busy, and out of the way. Just let Florence get on with it. Another few weeks and all the fame and notoriety of the programme will be over, and we can all go back to normal."

I grunted. What is normal at Whittle Inn, after all?

Charity produced a huge wad of letters, held together by a fat rubber band. "Why don't you take these up to the office and sort through them?"

I took the post from her with a grimace. "I expect most of these are for Florence. More fan mail. Is it ever going to stop?"

Charity looked confused. "Aren't there six episodes of this programme?"

"Yes, I believe so." I drifted towards the kitchen door and the back stairs to the next floor.

"Well, you'd better get used to it. Witchflix has only aired the first episode, so there's five more to come."

I had a wash and changed my grass-soiled robes for slightly cleaner ones before meandering through to my office. Gwyn, my long-deceased great-grandmother, hovered at the window, while Mr Hoo chirruped and twitted from his perch next to the fireplace. Thankfully Zephaniah, in Florence's absence, had set it ablaze for me. The nights were starting to draw in, with a tendency to be damp. A roaring fire made all the difference, but you needed to let a fire burn and settle before it would begin to give off a decent amount of heat and cheer.

I scratched Mr Hoo's head and he chirruped away happily; preening himself and shedding feathers and fluff all over the rug.

"Everything alright, Grandmama?" I asked, slipping the rubber band away from the letters to begin sorting through them.

"Yes, my dear," she answered. I cast a quick

glance her way, not convinced by her distracted response, but decided I didn't want to know. Trouble had a way of finding itself to the heart of my wonky inn and I could do without any more of it for the time being.

"Miss Florence Fidler." I placed the first letter down on the desk. "Miss Florence Fidler." Another one. "F. Fidler. Flo Fiddley. Gas bill. Gas bill again?" I absently sifted through the letters and created separate piles. "Florence. Ms F Fidler. The Ghost on Witchy Cake Off. Invoice from Whittle Stores." I nodded at Mr Hoo, who had paused in his grooming routine to watch me through his huge golden eyes. "That'll be all that flour we had to buy," I told him and tossed another couple of envelopes onto Florence's pile, before pausing.

A familiar style of envelope.

Red ink on fine quality stained parchment; the address written out in long hand, in a neat cursive handwriting.

I sighed.

It could only be Sabien Laurent, an old French vampire who had arranged a wedding for his hideous playboy son here at Whittle Inn, nearly twelve months before. Until they'd arrived in the dead of night, I'd had very little experience of vampires.

After the groom's escapades over the following week, I'd quickly decided I never wanted anything more to do with the nocturnal menaces ever again.

Nope. Never again. Uh uh. No way, Jose.

Sabien however seemed to have other plans. He insisted on writing to me. I never bothered opening the letters, merely burning or shredding them as they arrived on my desk.

Why write to me at all? I could only imagine that the wretched man desired a return visit. Or maybe he intended to put pressure on me to tell him the whereabouts of Marc Williams, a previously important member of Sabien's nest of vampires. Marc had broken free from Sabien's clutches after the horrible events during the previous October.

I'd never tell. I'd been sworn to secrecy and a witch's oath is sacrosanct.

Blowing out my cheeks in exasperation, I screwed the envelope up, but as I took aim to throw it into the fireplace, Mr Hoo shot off his perch and blocked the way, flapping his powerful wings and hovering in the air.

"Get out of the way, you great daft featherball," I told him, but he only fixed me with a determined glare. I frowned. This wasn't like him.

"What's up?" I asked.

"Hooo. Hoooo-ooo."

"You want me to open this?" I scowled.

He flapped his wings harder, sending loose papers and Florence's pile of fan mail fluttering across the floor. "Hoo!"

"Okay, okay," I said and gestured him out of the way. The second he shifted and made for his perch, I threw the balled-up envelope at the fire.

Quick as a flash he turned in mid-air and dived for the missile, heading straight for the flames. Seeing what would happen I shrieked in alarm. Without thinking I jumped to my feet and shot a spell his way. "*Impediendum.*" My little owl buddy froze where he was, the tip of one wing dangling just millimetres above the blaze. The envelope bounced off the grill and back onto the rug in front of the hearth. The slightly singed scent of burning feathers shocked me out of my daze and I quickly looped back the energy I'd sent, pulling it towards me so that Mr Hoo fell to the floor. He shook himself in indignation and twitted angrily at me.

"Are you crazy?" I squawked at him.

"Hoo! Hoo!"

"I am not!" I waggled my finger at him. "That's was a stupid stunt. You could have been seriously burned. You might have ended up like Florence.

That's the last thing I need, having the pair of you old nags haunting me together!" I bent over him to check for damage and he took aim at my finger with his sharp beak. "Ouch!"

He carried on twitting in indignation and shook himself before making a leap for his perch. I observed his movements, looking for the slightest hint of injury, until satisfied everything appeared to be normal. Then with a sigh of relief I rescued the scrunched-up envelope.

"So much drama," I grumbled, returning to my seat where I smoothed the envelope out on the desk. I cast a quick look at Mr Hoo. He in turn watched me.

I tutted, rolled my eyes and then ripped the envelope open to withdraw a single sheet of vellum.

The message was short and to the point.

Mademoiselle Daemonne

I have been trying to reach out to you but so far to no avail.

I have received word that you and your inn are in grave danger.

I would urge you and your guests to remove your-

selves from Whittlecombe forthwith. Seek safe harbour with Wizard Shadowmender. Lie low.

Je vous prie d'agréer, l'expression demes respectueux hommages.

Sabien Laurent

Chapter Two

"Ha. Ha. Ha." I sounded out each syllable separately, but I wasn't even remotely amused. The nerve of the man.

I read and re-read the message, frowning over the implied meaning behind the words. Was this a threat from a deranged vampire? Or could it be a genuine warning? I had no idea.

I noticed the quiet around me and looked up. Mr Hoo regarded me with a slightly wary, almost scared expression.

Gwyn, her back to the window so that I could see the faint outline of the trees beyond through her transparent form, stared at me with pursed lips.

What did they know? Why had Mr Hoo insisted I read the contents of the letter? Why was Gwyn fixing me with such a troubled look?

I opened my mouth and closed it again. I had no intention of paying lip service to the pointy-toothed miscreant from Paris.

Gwyn turned about to gaze out of the window again. She tilted her head slightly as though watching something. From where I sat, whatever it was remained out of my sight. A flitter of anxiety beat against the walls of my stomach and I couldn't resist it. I stood and made my way over to her. The sun would set soon, the sky hung overcast. We might finally have some rain.

I studied my great-grandmother's face in profile. Her expression seemed heavier than normal. Something weighty had settled upon her.

"Bats," she said.

"Bats?" I repeated.

"The past few evenings, I've seen them circling the inn."

I rubbed my temples. *Coincidence. That's all it was.*

"It's an old building," I said. "They tend to enjoy the rafters and the thatched roof, the turrets and the old wattle and daub..." I trailed off as Gwyn nodded. I could tell she wasn't convinced.

"The letter was from Sabien?" she asked.

I could hardly deny it. "Yes. But nothing to worry about."

Gwyn smirked. "Good try, Alfhild. I know when you're lying."

"Well, you can see for yourself." I gestured towards the desk where the letter lay. "He thinks there's some danger here."

"And you think not?"

I forced a laugh, hating how it sounded. "No, of course not. I admit I'm a little unnerved, but we've dealt with worse than a few crazy vampires in the past. I won't let them get to me."

"But it's not just about you, is it my dear?" Gwyn reminded me. "You have responsibilities."

"And I take them very seriously," I reminded her. "I do. I may not have in the past, but I do now."

Gwyn nodded. "I know you do."

We regarded each other in silence for a moment. If Gwyn was this unnerved then I owed it to her to listen to her misgivings. She'd been a mighty fine witch in her lifetime. In fact, she was a mighty fine witch after it.

I backed down. "I'll speak to Wizard Shadowmender. But honestly, I think this is all hot air and dandruff. Sabien is trying to intimidate me. He wants to know where Marc and Kat are."

"You don't know where they are," Gwyn replied, arching her eyebrows.

"Exactly. So it's a secret I can't help him with. When he understands that he'll back off."

"But you'll speak to Wizard Shadowmender anyway?"

"I'll do it now," I promised.

"I'd hate for us to be taken unawares." Gwyn glanced back out at the sky, evidently bat-spotting again.

"Let's not be overly concerned. We have an inn full of witches," I said, sounding more confident than I felt. "Think of the knowledge we have between us. And the spells! I'm sure we can cope with a few stray vampires."

Gwyn refused to be reassured that easily. "On the contrary. We shouldn't be complacent. What we have is an inn full of intrinsically good witches. I'm not sure how useful they would be under battle conditions."

She had a point.

"But we have Silvan," I countered. "He's worth a dozen vampires. And there's not much that's good about him either!"

I hadn't had to use the orb for a while. Guiltily, I pulled it from its box in my wardrobe and dusted it off before carrying it over to the window seat. I lifted it to catch the last rays of the sun and it sparkled with an almost effervescent energy before clouding over.

Holding it at chest height I stared into the glass, watching as the clouds dissipated, until they finally revealed Wizard Shadowmender's cheerful face with his ruddy cheeks, white hair and beard. "Greetings, Alf," he beamed. "Long time, no see!"

I smiled back at him. His cheerfulness and unrelenting positivity was infectious. "Greetings, Wizard Shadowmender. I apologise for not being in touch."

"Oh that's no problem. I know you've been very busy with the telly people. I hope that apart from the unfortunate murder of the producer, it was a success?"

"I think it was." I nodded. "Florence tells me the ratings are very good. She's obviously made up about how it's all turned out. She was the runner-up, you know?"

"So I heard. Such a clever young woman and a wonderful baker. I shall have to visit again soon and remind myself of just how talented she is."

"She will be thrilled to hear you say so. You're always welcome here, you know that."

I hesitated, needing to get to the crux of our conversation but unsure what to say. "There's something I need to share with you."

The elderly wizard nodded and settled back in his chair. I could see from the bookshelves behind him, and the various odd instruments on display, that he was at home in his little house in Surbiton. From the outside it looked like any ordinary and rather dull semi-detached, but once you entered, the place seemed to open out to the proportions of a small castle.

"Share away, share away," he instructed me.

I held up Sabien's letter. "I had this in the post today. It's from Sabien Laurent. You remember him?"

Wizard Shadowmender's eyes shone. He loved a little challenge. "I do." He cocked his head. "I take it he's not planning on booking a holiday with you?"

"I'd give him short shrift if he did," I said. "No. This is a warning. He says that both me and my inn are in danger."

"Hmm." Wizard Shadowmender frowned. "Does he give a reason?"

"No. Just tells me to empty the inn of guests and get to safety."

Wizard Shadowmender chuckled. "I'm guessing that's not on the cards, Alf?"

I wavered. "Well it wouldn't generally be something I would consider—"

"But?"

"But both my great-grandmother and Mr Hoo are uneasy." Putting this into words underlined how unusual I found this. "I trust them. Mr Hoo stays out of the way of vampires, and Grandmama, well... you know what a formidable force she is."

"Indeed." Wizard Shadowmender considered what I'd said. "This is most odd. I've had no intelligence about anything afoot, so I'm not sure what to suggest."

That wasn't particularly helpful.

"However... I think in light of your great-grandmother's misgivings, perhaps we should take the threat seriously."

"I'm not leaving Whittle Inn—"

Wizard Shadowmender held up one hand. "Peace, Alf. I'm not suggesting you do. But perhaps you should close to guests for a few days until we've had a chance to put some feelers out. I can pass on what you've told me to Penelope and her team of wizards and see what they discover."

Reluctantly I nodded. I could see the logic of this approach.

"I wouldn't normally pander to someone like Sabien, I must admit," Wizard Shadowmender continued, "but a threat to your guests? That I think we must take seriously."

I had to agree.

"You haven't noticed anything out of the ordinary of late?" Wizard Shadowmender asked and I shook my head. I'd been too busy eating cake and conjuring djinns to pay attention to the real world.

"No." I could have kicked myself for becoming so complacent. "Nothing at all. But to be honest, this isn't the first letter Sabien has sent me over the past few months. I haven't opened any of the others."

"Sometimes danger comes from unexpected sources," Wizard Shadowmender said. "We don't always see it coming." He clapped his hands to dispel my misgivings. "Not to worry, Alf. We'll get to the bottom of it. Send me a copy of that letter. CC it into Penelope too if you don't mind."

"I will do. I'll close the inn and cancel any bookings for the next week or so as well."

"An excellent idea. Keep in touch." Wizard Shadowmender clicked his fingers and flicked a spark at his own orb. The spark grew in size and obliterated his face, and then the glass was clear once more leaving me staring at the ghost of my own reflection.

I became aware of voices on the lawn outside. Frau Krauss, a frequent visitor to the inn was returning from a walk in Speckled Wood. Finbarr, my young Irish witch friend, scampered along beside her. Frau Krauss was tall, and he was short, and the pair looked comical together. Of his annoying pixies there was no sign.

She was one of many guests who loved to stay here at Whittle Inn.

I sighed. I hated to close the inn when we were full of visitors. I'd have to elicit Charity's help. She would manage the situation much better than I. Maybe we could arrange a free return visit or negotiate discounts for future bookings. In the meantime, I needed to make a few dozen phone calls and postpone any reservations we'd taken for the next few weeks leading up to Halloween.

A thought occurred to me as I returned the orb to its box and stowed it safely away in the wardrobe. What if this was all an elaborate hoax and all Sabien wanted to do was damage my reputation?

I sniffed. Well if that was the case, I'd create a

hex that would be so powerful, he'd rue the day he messed with me and threatened my wonky inn.

In the meantime, it was evidently better to be safe than sorry.

I closed the wardrobe and made my way purposefully to my office.

Time to let folks down gently.

CHAPTER THREE

"How did your high tea go yesterday?" Florence and I were making up packed-lunch boxes for all our guests. Many of them had long journeys to take in order to get home. In addition to some homegrown witchy guests from all corners of the British Isles, we had a few Salem witches visiting, along with two from Florida, one from Chile, one from Russia, and Frau Krause of course. A most international contingent of magickal folk.

"Very well, thank you, Miss Alf." Florence piped a layer of buttercream onto some cupcakes with studied concentration. I didn't really see the point myself. No cupcake ever managed to get out of a lunch box without taking some damage. It didn't matter how pretty the piping was right now, a mile down the road and it would look like it had been chucked at a wall.

"That's good news." I tried to sound bouncy, but I have to admit I was feeling a little low. I pulled a tin from the cupboard near me. It contained two-day old brownies and blondies. "Maybe we should give them these rather than cupcakes? What do you think, Florence?"

Florence blinked at me pointedly, her cheeks covered as they always were in soot, while smoke floated above her head from her singed clothing. "I've made cupcakes now, Miss Alf."

"I'd just hate for them to get squashed after all your work."

"They'll still be edible." Florence smiled at me; the smile a parent gives a child when they know better.

"Alright."

"We can give them a brownie as well if you like, Miss Alf. There's plenty to go around." Florence was humouring me, but it did make me a feel a little more useful as I carefully wrapped brownies in wax paper and slipped them inside the cardboard boxes lined up on the table.

Monsieur Emietter was busy buttering bread and layering sandwiches. Somewhere, probably in the bar, Charity was organising Zephaniah and Ned who were acting as bell boys and rounding up bags, cases, broomsticks, hat boxes, potion cases, knitting baskets, as well as cages and carrycases containing familiars. Everything needed to be loaded onto the small coach we'd hired to take everyone into Exeter. The idea was that one vehicle would save on taxis and ease the transfer to other onward transport services.

"Miss Alf, how long do you intend to close the inn for exactly?" Florence asked as she carefully pimped the last cupcake.

"Hopefully just a few days," I said. I had yet to hear back from Wizard Shadowmender. I could imagine Ross Baines and his technical wizard colleagues holed up in a dark basement somewhere—at the behest of Penelope Quigwell—searching for clues as to what the vampires were up to.

"Well the timing is very good..." Florence avoided my curious gaze.

"Is it? Good for what?" I flipped down a couple of lids on the boxes and began labelling them 'vege', 'vegan' and 'meat'.

"One of the women who came to my high tea yesterday was from a publishing company. They want me to write a book for them."

Argh! I knew it! I was going to lose Florence to the celebrity circuit. She'd have her own TV show on Witchflix and maybe even the Beeb, and before I knew it she'd be in a jungle eating witchity-grubs or rocking a bikini on an island somewhere looking for faux love. Then Whittle Inn would be a housekeeper down and who would make all my cakes? And…

I reined in my panic.

"Gosh. That's a big step."

"Do you think it's a step too far, Miss Alf?" The note of worry in her tone had me regretting my selfish response. I stopped what I was doing so I could look at her properly.

"No of course not. You have the most amazing and creative ideas. You'll produce a wonderful book. Everybody will want a copy."

Florence dipped her head in embarrassment. "Oh that's kind of you, Miss."

"Is this a reputable publisher?" I asked. "You need to be careful about how much they offer and how much they take in royalties and stuff. I've heard that many of the big publishers take a huge cut and it doesn't leave much for the person that did all the work."

"Quite a big publisher. Fatto and Windup. They publish both Faery Kerry and Raoul Scurrysnood's books. It was Raoul who recommended me apparently."

She dropped the names into the conversation like confetti. Such celebrated circles my housekeeper had started to move in. It wasn't that long ago I'd taken her up to London for the first time, now here she was courting the big publishing houses.

"They recommended I find myself an agent who'll hammer out a deal on my behalf." The way she was speaking, like she knew what she was doing, quite took my breath away. "They gave me a list of names to try but that means accessing the internet or using the phone."

That kind of summed up Florence in a nutshell. She was a wonderful baker, superlative in fact, and here she was being headhunted by a publisher, and yet she didn't know how to work a telephone or a computer.

But then why should she? Neither of those had been invented while she was alive.

In fact the inn hadn't even had electricity back then.

"I'll help you," I promised. "I'm not going to have much to do over the next few days."

"What? You're not staying here, are you?" Charity had overheard the tail end of the conversation. She had brought down a load of used towels from the bedrooms upstairs. "I thought you said everybody had to leave."

"I'm not everybody though, am I?" I shrugged. "I'm the owner. I have to stay. The Captain of the ship doesn't desert her bridge."

"Well I want to stay with you," Charity insisted. "You can't be here by yourself. What if someone does come looking for you?"

"I won't be here by myself." I indicated Florence. "All of the ghosts will be here."

"But what sort of protection are they?" Charity complained and I suppose to a certain extent she had a point.

"I have Gwyn," I reminded her.

Charity shook her head. "If I recall correctly, the last time the vampires came anywhere near here, Gwyn disappeared."

I pouted. That was true. "Where does she go?" I asked, more to myself than to anyone else, but both Charity and Florence shrugged in unison.

"Have you tried asking her?" Charity tightened her grip on her towels as one or two of them tried to escape the bundle.

"Of course. She won't tell me though." I chewed the inside of my lip. Would Gwyn stick around until

Wizard Shadowmender gave us the all clear or not? "It doesn't matter anyway," I asserted as I turned my attention to labelling the boxes once more. "I'll be fine. Silvan isn't going anywhere."

"What do you mean you're going back to London?"

Silvan and I walked out into the drive. Gwyn, Florence, Charity, Zephaniah and Ned were already waving off our guests. We'd piled the old Devon General coach high with miscellaneous belongings and familiars, and presented each with a packed lunch box, then hugged and commiserated, consoled, laughed and high-fived depending on each individual guest's specific penchant or needs. Now we stood outside the inn like some kind of modern-day Adams Family and waved them away. The old green coach, a relic from the 1950s and now on hire from a local transport company, lumbered slowly and noisily down the drive that led to Whittle Lane and Whittlecombe, disappearing from view between the oak trees, leaving a trail of stinky black smoke in its wake.

My colleagues made themselves scarce as I confronted Silvan, although I noticed Charity grimacing when she noticed us bickering, as she walked backwards away from us.

"You can't go now!" I cried and Silvan held his hands up in mock surrender.

"Alf, it's not my first choice, believe me. But you know I have to make a living and I've been hired to do a job."

"What job?" I snapped, feeling infinitely annoyed.

Silvan reached out to take my hand, but I quickly pulled it away. "It doesn't matter 'what job'," he said. "I'm a witch-for-hire. I go where I'm needed. To the person who pays me the most."

He couldn't go. I didn't want him to.

"I'll pay you. What will it cost me?"

Silvan's eyes met mine and he smiled, a gentle knowing smile that hurt my heart. "I'll never take money from you, Alfhild."

I glowered at him. "You did once."

"Well that was before I knew you. And now that I do know you, everything is different."

"Is it?" *How is it different?* I wanted to ask.

"It is," Silvan repeated firmly. "Look. I will go and attend to the business calling me to Tumble Town and then I'll come back as soon as I can. I promise."

"How long will that be?" I asked, and I heard the note of fear in my voice, the tremor in my tone. How ridiculous. I was a grown woman; a powerful witch. I didn't need a man, any man, let alone this abominable rogue.

Silvan laughed. I swear blind that the dirty rat could read my mind at times. "It will take as long as it takes, you know that."

Of course it would. I had to admit defeat. Silvan was going back to Tumble Town and I might not see him for months. Gwyn would disappear. I could only hope that Wizard Shadowmender would get to the bottom of the threat against Whittle Inn very quickly,

I spun on my heel and marched back into the inn.

"Alf? Don't be like that," Silvan called after me. "Where are you going? Alf?"

"I'm going to the kitchen," I shouted over my shoulder. "I suppose you'll be wanting a packed lunch too."

He left an hour later. We called a taxi specially to take him to an Exeter train station.

"You could have just gone on the coach with everyone else," I grumped at him as we hovered by the open passenger door. He didn't have much in the way of luggage. He'd arrived here with his friend Marissa for a weekend and stayed on a little while longer.

"I could have done," Silvan said. "But then I'd have had to share a goodbye with everyone else."

"What makes you think I'm going to give you a send-off that's any different to anyone else's?" I asked. He leaned in towards me, his dark, dark eyes burning through mine; into my very soul. My stomach turned cartwheels at our proximity. He smelled of toothpaste and shampoo, mixed with something a little musky. Not unpleasant. For a fraction of a second, I wanted to fall into his embrace. Then I remembered who I was dealing with. *A woman in every town. A port in every storm.* I backed away. "You're not going to kiss me, are you?"

"Would that be so terrible?" His voice purred with desire.

"Yes," I said and moved to push him away. He caught my hands easily, folded them together and brought them to his mouth. He chuckled at the sight of my face, kissed each of my thumbs in turn and winked before dropping my hands and straightening up.

"Very well," he said. "As you wish." He placed one hand on the roof of the car and almost climbed in but stopped and turned back to me once more. "Alf?" He hesitated. "Perhaps you should ask George to come and stay here. Until I can get back."

I screwed my face up, wondering what particular variety of mushrooms Silvan had eaten for his breakfast. "George?" Inviting my detective ex to stay at the inn was not a good idea. "I can't do that. What about Stacey?"

Stacey. Ugh. I could barely say her name without wanting to cause serious damage to someone or something. George and I had enjoyed a good thing until she poked her pretty little snub nose into our affairs.

"Well invite her over too. Maybe some old sugar-daddy of a vampire will find her... appetising?" Silvan winked and climbed into his seat.

As he pulled the door closed and wound the window down I came closer to stand alongside him. I bent down and smiled. "That's a terrible idea."

He reached through the window and stroked my cheek with a warm hand. I didn't complain. "I'll be back as soon as I can. Stay safe until then, Alfie."

I wanted his hand to stay there forever, keeping me safe. "You too," I replied and stepped back towards the inn as the car ambled away, spitting chips of granite as it went.

I watched him disappear from my view, and suddenly my heart felt hollow.

What a frightfully annoying being he was.

CHAPTER FOUR

"Only me!" Millicent's voice echoed around the empty bar. "Anyone home?"

I trotted in from the kitchen where I'd been searching for a cheese grater and looked at my friend in surprise. In her sixties, and a proud member of the Whittlecombe WI, Millicent was the unlikeliest of witches. Today she was wearing a pair of red tartan trousers with a yellow blouse and a completely clashing fuchsia pink scarf. She looked like some kind of demented Rupert the Bear tribute act. I'd lost count of the amount of times I'd started our conversations with, "Just *what* are you wearing?"

Fortunately she never took umbrage and I loved her like a second mother.

"What are you doing here?" I rushed over to give her a hug.

"Charity popped her head in on her way home to her mother's and told me you'd banished her."

"It wasn't like that," I began to protest.

"Well I knew you couldn't have possibly wanted to be here all alone. I mean, that would be ridiculous. So we decided to come and wait with you?"

"We?" I assumed she meant the dogs, Jasper the lurcher and Sunny the Yorkie. I could hear barking out on the lawn. Zephaniah would not be pleased if they were busy fertilising his hard work.

"Yoo hoo!" Charity burst in behind Millicent while the dogs yapped, wagging and dancing and generally doing what excited dogs do, as they chased into the bar.

"Charity!" I scolded her.

"Ah-ah!" She wagged her finger at me. "Don't give me any lip. See, I'm in civvies." She had changed into calf-length jeans, a casual t-shirt and trainers, and had bound her hair up in a handkerchief, with just her shocking blonde quiff poking out. She looked like a 1950s rockabilly chick.

"You shouldn't—"

"Work Alf instructed Work Charity to leave the inn for her own safety. But Friend Charity and Friend Millicent think Lonely Friend Alf needs company. So here we are. You can't turn your well-meaning friends away."

I was outnumbered. "Alright, alright. I know when I'm beaten." I tutted in exasperation and gestured towards the kitchen. "I was just making cheese on toast. Does anyone want some?"

Millicent looked at me in distaste. "Cheese on toast? For dinner? Where's Monsieur Emietter?"

"I gave him some time off." I'd thought it a waste of his talent simply to cater for me and Finbarr.

"And where's Florence?" Charity asked.

I pointed at the ceiling. Florence would be in the attic. "Writing her book."

"Her book?" Millicent asked. Charity evidently hadn't filled Millicent in on all the details.

"Our Florence may be in line for a publishing deal with one of the big London publishers," I explained. "So I'm afraid I'm cooking dinner, and erm… cheese on toast is my speciality."

Millicent shook her head. "Looks like I'm taking over in the kitchen then. Good job I brought supplies with me!"

Millicent's supplies were an absolute goddess-send. She'd had the foresight to bring a basket full of late-ripening tomatoes from her greenhouse along with some onions. Now she quickly set a tomato, onion and basil soup to simmer on the stove while I crushed some garlic to mix with cheese and butter to make cheesy-garlic bread. Who knew I had such culinary skills?

"No word from Wizard Shadowmender yet?" Charity was sitting at the kitchen table watching Millicent and I work.

"Nope. Not yet." I wrapped my garlic bread in foil and stood it on a baking tray, before checking to see whether the oven was actually on. My prowess in the kitchen often didn't get much further than being thwarted by the on/off switch.

"No news is good news, right?" Charity asked.

"I suppose so." I glanced from her to Millicent. "Why is it taking so long to get back to me, though?"

Millicent stirred the soup. "You're thinking they're struggling to find anything out?"

I nodded. "I know Penelope and her technical wizards. They can discover anything about anybody and they're usually pretty fast. If they can't see what the vampires in Sabien's nest are up to, or where they are, then that can't really be a good thing, can it?"

"You're assuming that the danger stems from Sabien, then?" Millicent blew on her wooden spoon and brought the mixture to her lips to taste it.

"Of course. You remember him. He was a total—"

"His son was worse." Charity shuddered.

"Melchior? Yes he was."

"It seems a huge assumption to me, Alf. Why would Sabien warn you?" Millicent asked. "If he intended to do you harm, surely he'd have just got on with it."

I shrugged. I had no idea, but she had a point.

Charity screwed up her face, thinking hard, while Millicent and I lapsed into silence as we worked on dinner. Suddenly she slammed her hand down on the table, scaring Sunny who had been sleeping underneath it. "Hey! Perhaps it's Melchior who's actually behind it, but Sabien caught wind of what he was up to and decided to warn you?"

I supposed that was feasible. "Maybe. They were as thick as thieves. That's all I know." I threw the baking tray into the oven and slammed the door with more force than it warranted. Simply the thought of Melchior and Sabien ruffled my feathers.

"Here." Millicent poked around in the big jute bag she had brought with her. "This will cheer you up." She hooked out a pair of clear wine bottles, full of pink liquid.

"Oooh Mills!" Charity cooed. "Is this what I think it is?"

"My own home-brewed rhubarb wine. Yes indeed." Millicent looked very pleased with herself.

I eyed the wine with suspicion. "Bad-heads-are-us in the morning then."

"Oh don't be such a misery, Alf." Charity elbowed me in the ribs. "It may have escaped your notice, but we don't have to get up tomorrow. We haven't any guests to see to."

This thought cheered me immensely. "In that case, let's go through to the bar and set a table. Party time!"

When you get to a certain age, hangovers become more difficult to shake off. I'd worked in hospitality my entire adult life, so I had grown used to a drink or two. Recently though, I'd begun to feel that I'd rather stay sober than fight through the challenges a day at the inn tended to throw up. The memory of my most recent overindulgence whilst enjoying the company of Silvan and Stacey and George all at the same time—and let's face it, wouldn't you have overindulged as well?—had left a sour taste in my mouth in more ways than one. As a result, I eased my foot off the gas pedal and just had two small glasses of Millicent's medicinal wine and left Millicent and Charity to drink the lion's share.

We supped our fill of soup, nibbling at my garlic bread, and sat in the bar until nearly midnight. Many of the inn's ghosts came to join us, and in the soporific aftermath of our delicious supper, I found myself oddly moved to watch them as they interacted with the bar just as they would have done while alive. The Devonshire Fellows played some quiet music while Gwyn held court at the bar. Zephaniah and Ned leaned against it chatting quietly with others who had also come before and were now gone from this plane.

Charity, Millicent and I picked up on the quiet, thoughtful mood and found ourselves reminiscing with great fondness about previous guests and people we knew in the village. Between the pair of them, they lifted my spirits no end.

I waved them away with some regret. They could have stayed over but Millicent wanted to get back because of the dogs. I'd offered to call them a taxi, but really the village wasn't far, and the air would help restore some sobriety in theory. I sent Ned with them and of course Jasper and Sunny were perfectly able companions—mainly because they hadn't been on the sauce, unlike the rest of us.

Going up to bed in a mostly empty inn felt peculiar. Normally I would be able to sense the buzz of several dozen other beings, as they went about their lives. Many of my guests would stay up all night, playing cards, working magick, drinking in the bar or enjoying programmes on Witchflix. Others, like me, preferred the daytime. They'd be in their pyjamas and snoring by the time I was ready to hit the sack.

But this evening there was nothing. No sound and no movement. Just a quiet inn. Even my ghosts had drifted away. I climbed the stairs, the only noise the creak of the floorboards beneath my own feet.

I paused at my bedroom door, cocking my head to listen; basking in the silence. With a smile I pushed gently against the door, walked into my room...

... and frowned.

Mr Hoo perched on the edge my iron bedstead, busily chittering to Gwyn.

"I think you might be right," she was saying to

him. "But you know what my great-granddaughter is like."

"Erm, hello?" I made myself known to the conniving pair by pushing the door open wide and allowing it to clatter against the wall.

"Oh hello, dear. Your friends have decided to head home, have they?"

"Yes." I frowned at Gwyn's attempt to distract me from the conversation. "What are you two discussing?"

"You can still hear them walking down the lane." Gwyn blithely ignored my question.

I mooched over to where she floated by the open window. You could hear singing coming from somewhere, but I couldn't have sworn the voices were those of Millicent and Charity.

Or even that they were female.

"That might be the Devonshire Fellows," I said.

"Have you banished them to Speckled Wood again?" Gwyn asked.

"Hooo-ooo. Hooo-ooo."

"Stop ganging up on me you two." I went to draw the curtains, which I rarely did because it hindered Mr Hoo's free passage in and out of the inn, but Gwyn stopped me.

"There they are again." Something in her quiet

voice alerted me to a perceived danger. I leaned closer to the glass to try and follow where she was looking. At first I couldn't see anything in the dark sky, but eventually, when my eyesight adjusted to the moonlight, I saw exactly what she was seeing. Tiny black shapes flitting awkwardly around the grounds.

"Bats." I wanted to shrug it off as I had before, but now that my senses were on high alert I found I couldn't do it so easily.

The thing is, bats aren't unusual, especially in the country and in large old houses with dodgy thatched roofs. We might even have had a few before. Perhaps I'd never noticed.

But then again, didn't it stand to reason that if I'd never noticed them, maybe we hadn't actually had any in residence in the eighteen months I'd been the owner of the inn?

"What should we do?" I asked my great-grandmother.

Without a second's hesitation she apparated away, disappearing entirely from the room. "Grandmama?" I called, hoping she hadn't disappeared for the foreseeable future as I'd already predicted, leaving me alone with my potential vampire problem.

"Hooo-oooo. Hoo hoo-oooooh."

"What do you mean she's helping?" I asked my little owl buddy in frustration. "How is scooting off and leaving us here helping me?"

"Hooo. Hooooo." Mr Hoo fluttered his enormous wings and leapt gracefully to settle beside me at the window. He leaned over the edge and I reached out automatically, as though to prevent him plunging down. Soft, wispy light at ground level caught my eye.

Gwyn.

She strolled along the edge of the drive almost casually, peering up into the sky, her wand pulled out but held loosely in her hand.

"What is she doing?" I asked, more to myself than Mr Hoo.

"Hooo-oooo," he replied. *Minding 'our' business*, he said. I pulled a face, but he was right. I couldn't just leave our business to my long-deceased great-grandmother.

I followed Gwyn out into the garden, but I had to go the long way, down the stairs, along the back passage, through the inn and out of the front door. By the time I'd arrived on the front drive, Gwyn had disappeared around the side of the inn to where I kept Jed's van parked up.

I found her standing about twenty yards back from the inn, staring up at one of the turrets.

"The little blighters are trying to get in up there. Do you see?"

Tiny black shapes flitted backwards and forwards, battering their wings against an area of the roof I couldn't quite see in the darkness.

"How do we know they're not getting inside?" I asked. "They may have a nest in there already."

"Alfhild, credit me with some sixth sense. I'd know and so would Finbarr. He may seem obsessed with the perimeters of Speckled Wood, but he's much more security minded than you realise."

This was true. Ever since the episode where The Mori had found their way into the inn through a deep well in the beer cellar, we'd been more than fastidious about security at the inn. Finbarr was a huge part of keeping us safe, helped in large part by Mr Kephisto, a wizard who ran a bookshop in the neighbouring town of Abbotts Cromleigh. Mr Kephisto had created the original forcefield around the boundaries of the inn and my land and had gone on to become a useful ally and a wise and knowledgeable consultant.

"Then they're not getting in." I folded my arms

and glared at the turret as though my own indignation would keep the inn and its inhabitants safe.

"Really, Alfhild? Your naivety scares me at times." Gwyn sniffed. "Hasn't Silvan drilled it out of you yet?"

I looked askance at my great-grandmother, but she merely raised her officious eyebrows without making further comment. It constantly surprised me how much she seemed to approve of Silvan as a person. As a dark witch, with numerous shady practises and pastimes, and dubious ways of making a living, I would have thought she'd despise him. But they rubbed along together very well.

That made me suspicious of them both of course.

Or that's what I told myself.

"You think they will get in?" I looked back at the turret in alarm.

"Hush a second, child." Gwyn gently lifted her wand and pointed it directly at the area of thatch the bats were worrying. A thread of cool yellow-tinged, white light threaded its way slowly through the space between Gwyn and the roof. When the tip of the light made contact with the thatch, it slid like a snake, in and over itself, threading round and round and over and over, the way you might darn a hole in a sock.

The light glowed a brighter yellow, then orange, and finally a burning red, like the centre of a hot fire. I almost began to worry that Gwyn would set the roof alight, but at last she dropped her wand and the colour cooled until it only glowed gently in the darkness.

The bats seemed confused and darted at the roof with angry intent before fluttering away, circling and gathering momentum, and then trying again.

"They had obviously located our weak spot," Gwyn said. "I'll have Finbarr check out the eaves at first light."

"Good idea," I said, suddenly yawning. I couldn't help myself.

"You should get some sleep, Alfhild—"

Out of the corner of my eye I saw something heading towards me, too fast for me to react. I half turned, but it was upon me. A missile from above. It smacked the side of my forehead with such force it knocked me backwards a few feet. I groaned in surprise and tried to stand upright, but whatever it was launched itself at me again, snagging itself in my hair, digging its claws into my scalp and beating at me.

I shrieked in a very un-witchy way and tried to grab whatever it was, my fingers sliding against leathery, thin wings. It scratched at me, drawing blood, but every time I thought I had purchase it evaded my panicky hands by slipping free of my grasp.

Gwyn had her wand levelled, but something held her back. Perhaps she feared hitting me instead of the creature, or it may have been the fact that bats were dive-bombing her too. Of course they couldn't touch her, and only soared straight through her. One or two tumbled to the ground and the rest merely flew in a huge arc and came back for another go.

I finally got a hold of the thing tangled in my hair just as another one hurled itself at my eye. Fearing for my eyesight, I let go of the one on my head and grabbed a firm hold of the eye-thief. I heard the beating of wings growing thunderous and found myself knocked to the ground once more, as the bat burrowing at my face was dislodged. A thin eerie shriek had the back of my neck quivering, then my hair was wrenched painfully one last time. I closed my eyes, and rolled onto my front, covering my head to protect it. Objects fell out of the sky, hitting the ground close by, as light as conkers dropping from a chestnut tree. Something slimy landed on the back of my legs and I kicked it away in disgust.

The call of a hunting owl chilled my blood. What new horror was this? But pushing myself to my knees and looking around, I quickly realised the owl was Mr Hoo. Gwyn had lit the tip of her wand and I could see the devastation around me. Dead bats everywhere. Beheaded, dismembered, de-winged. Mr Hoo had enjoyed himself at least.

He flew several metres above the ground, circling around, staring at me through gold eyes that glinted with anger.

"Good job." I waved up at him, my voice slightly shaky, my knees trembling. The moon had disappeared behind some clouds, lending a strange silvery glow to the cumulus above.

"Alfhild, do you never carry your wand with you?" My great-grandmother scolded me and with good reason. Silvan would have said exactly the same thing.

"I—" I started to make an excuse about how I'd been enjoying a fun time with friends and had been intending to head for bed when a groan from behind us made me jump.

I spun about. Movement in the shadows to the side of the inn, near the tall hedgerow that separated my land from farmland, drew my attention. Warily I crept forwards, holding my breath, my hands out in front of me to deliver a defence spell if needed. Gwyn floated next to me; her wand held out in front with similar intent. Mr Hoo continued to circle overhead, watching proceedings.

The moon came out again and illuminated the ground. Something pale slid away from us, groaning in pain. I stared with morbid fascination as we drew closer. Whatever it was—half man, half-bat—it was grievously injured. One human arm, one wing, one human leg, one strange twisted bat foot.

I grimaced, unsure whether to reach for it and try to help it or leave it. But Gwyn made the decision for me. She lifted her wand and directed a bright ball of cold energy its way. "*Altera vita frui!*"

The thing had just enough time to fix me with one fevered eye and then he was jolted from this life. As I looked on in horror, his body began to dry and shrivel, tighter and tighter, imploding in on itself, until it was nothing more than ash. With a soft crump, the corpse exploded, dust flying everywhere.

I backed away from the grim sight, my lip curled, my stomach rolling, a disturbing memory rearing its ugly head.

Twelve months ago... while I'd been hosting the wretched vampire wedding at Whittle Inn... a vampire had been cruelly finished off in the bar. At the time, we'd been blamed even though we'd had nothing to do with the murder.

Without doubt, I knew the incident was connected to this sudden attack. This had to be the reason why the inn was currently under threat.

Yes, it had been a while, but revenge is a dish that is best served cold. Isn't that what they say?

Somebody somewhere was dying to find out...

Just who had killed Thaddeus?

CHAPTER FIVE

I couldn't have been in bed for longer than an hour when some horrendous clanking noise woke me.

I sat bolt up in bed, my heart beating hard in my chest listening to the deep growling sound originating from out the front of the inn. It rumbled and clunked, not a monster as I'd first thought, but oddly mechanical. This time I remembered to reach for my wand as I swung my legs out of bed.

I glanced at the pitch-black sky through the open window. The clock by the side of my bed informed me the time was 3.37 a.m. Mr Hoo was nowhere to be seen.

"Gwyn?" I called softly and she appeared immediately at the end of my bed.

"Did you need me, Alfhild?"

"Can you hear that?"

"I should imagine the whole of Whittlecombe can hear it, Alfhild. Why don't you go and see what they want at this time of night?"

I blinked at my great-grandmother in confusion. We'd been fighting off vampires a few hours ago and now she wanted me to head downstairs in my nightshirt and confront whatever new terror threatened the inn? I crept towards the window, a little reluctantly I must admit. My body hurt in various places, most especially my head where my hair had been yanked, and my face where the bat had tried to burrow into my eye. I gently brushed hair from my forehead and peeped out into the grounds.

A Volkswagen camper van had been parked in front of the inn's main entrance, its engine still idling noisily. Its headlight picked out the light drizzle but blinded me enough that I couldn't see the occupants inside. Even as I watched, the passenger door swung open, and a fair-haired man jumped out. He crossed in front of the campervan, ducking against the rain as though that would keep him dry, and knocked hard on the front door.

The sound of his calling reverberated deeply throughout the inn, and I sensed the sudden disturbance as dozens of ghosts stirred or glanced warily about.

While it is highly unusual in this day and age for people to simply turn up at the inn on the off chance of a room without some sort of reservation, it isn't totally unheard of. That's what inns are for after all. They offer succour in the deep of the night. That's especially true of my paranormal hostelry. It comes with the territory.

Groaning, and knowing full well I was the only mortal at home and therefore the only being who could physically unlock the front door—locked and bolted after the run-in with the bats a few hours earlier—I slipped on my dressing gown and slowly made my way down the stairs.

The thunderous knocking came again. The front door of the inn, made from solid aged oak wood, has a heavy brass knocker and was designed, literally, to wake the dead. When you grab it and hit the wood hard, it certainly makes a great deal of noise. Especially at half three in the morning when there are no bodies around to soak up the sound.

We had increased security of all the doors and windows after the final skirmish we'd had with The Mori back in May, so now I used a combination of human methods and a touch of witchy enchantment to lock up at night. I drew back the bolts, one after the other, top, bottom and middle, and fiddled with the double lock.

From outside, the knock came again, ensuring my already aching head throbbed painfully. "Okay, okay, I'm here. Give me a minute," I called.

I eventually managed to align the locks in the right order. The final part of the puzzle was a spell. I touched each lock in turn, a single spark flying from my fingers whenever they made contact with the iron, and then muttered, "*Ingressum.*" Something deep inside the wood of the door clicked—the signal that it could now be opened.

With a simple turn of the handle, I pulled the door towards myself but stopped it with a well-positioned foot and my shoulder.

"I'm sorry," I began as soon as I'd opened it a crack, not really taking in the figure sheltering from the wet weather. "I'm afraid Whittle Inn is closed for a few days—"

"Alf? It's me. Let us in."

I blinked at the tall man in front of me. His face was as pale as it had ever been, but his short, previously badly self-cut hair had grown down to his shoulders. His light blue eyes sparkled with happy life. "Marc?"

Marc Williams, the vampire who'd won the heart

of Melchior Laurent's intended, Ekaterina Lukova when Whittle Inn had hosted the infamous vampire wedding twelve months previously, stood peering in at me through pale, guileless eyes. In light of Melchior's subsequent fury, and threats against Ekaterina's family, Wizard Shadowmender had granted Marc and Kat safe passage and they had remained in hiding, well away from Melchior and his friends, for nearly twelve months.

So what were they doing here?

"Yes! It's me, Marc. And Kat's here too." He gestured over his shoulder at the rusty battered Volkswagen which still grumbled away to itself on the drive. I peered out. Kat spotted me looking her way and waved, a huge grin on her face.

"No." I said and reeled back in horror.

"No?" Marc asked in confusion.

"You can't be here. You *can't*!"

Marc frowned. "I thought you'd be happy to see us."

"I'm not. I mean I am. But no. You shouldn't be here. Why have you come?"

Marc laughed. He'd always been such a good-natured positive soul. A friendly vegan, he made for a really appalling vampire. "You are a big silly, Alf. You invited us. Remember?"

"I didn't."

We sat at the bar nursing a small brandy each. I studied my hands, battered and bleeding from my recent batty encounter. I needed a bath.

The Volkswagen had been hastily parked beside Jed's van and I'd quickly escorted Kat and Marc inside the safety of the inn and locked the whole place down once more. I'd sent Zephaniah to get word to Finbarr. The security of the inn and its new guests was of even greater importance now.

"We had a letter," Marc insisted, and Kat dug around in her bag until she could find a crumpled sheet of A4. The letter, printed using modern means, *had* been signed in my name, but electronically and not by hand. Certainly not by my hand. An electronic signature was not something I would ever do.

I stared at the headed notepaper. It had a Whittle Inn motif that Charity had designed when she'd first arrived as manager, but the paper we used was thicker and embossed. This image had been scanned.

I lay the paper down on top of the bar and stared at it for some time, my eyes gritty with lack of sleep.

There were no obvious clues as to whom had sent this, but it had to be a set up.

Marc and Kat had been lured to an inn, now almost devoid of the people who might have been able to protect them.

"Is everything alright, Alf?" Kat's thick accent cut through my troubled thoughts. Originating in Chernoistochinsk in Russia, she was one of the most beautiful women I had ever met. Lustrous long dark hair and a perfectly composed face, but she hardly knew the power of her own beauty. She'd almost married Melchior when he had blackmailed her into doing so by threatening her family, but when the opportunity had presented itself she had dropped him like a hot brick.

And love, I'd witnessed first-hand, has a way of winning out. Marc, who had adored Kat from afar, had won her heart.

I gazed at them thoughtfully, wondering how marriage between a mortal and a vampire was working out for them both. Unless Kat had been turned....

I winced. But it was none of my business.

"Only... you look like... what's the saying, Marc? You have been hauled out of the bushes from behind." She smiled, pleased with herself.

"Dragged through a hedge backwards," Marc corrected her, smiling. "Yes. You do." He directed this latter comment at me, so I pouted at him.

"That's probably because I was attacked by a bunch of psycho bats tonight." I gently patted my left eyelid which was hot to the touch. I'd bathed it of course, but figured I'd have to wait until morning to see what the damage was. Maybe I'd give Millicent a shout and she could blend some potion that would aid a swift recovery. She was good at stuff like that.

"Bats?" Marc repeated, his face falling. I could see he understood the issue straightaway.

I nodded. "You're not the only one to have had a letter. I heard from Sabien a few days ago. He wrote to me warning me that I was in danger. In fact, not just me, but everyone staying at the inn. So, after talking to Wizard Shadowmender I agreed to send everyone away. It's just me and Finbarr here, plus the ghosts. Everyone else has gone."

"All the guests?" Kat glanced around in wide-eyed wonder. Not that many of my guests would have been up at this time anyway, but of course the bar was completely deserted.

"And Charity too." I pointed out of the window into the darkness. "Then tonight Grandmama became even more concerned about the bats. She suggested there were more of them than ever and that they were more active. I thought it was just one of those things. Turns out there were *dozens* of them trying to find their way into the inn."

"But they didn't manage that?" Kat looked distinctly queasy now.

"No. Thanks to Grandmama."

"And they attacked you?" Marc asked, doubtfully.

I pointed at my face. "I didn't do this to myself now, did I?"

"No, no of course you didn't." Marc tried to backtrack. "It's just unusual—from my experience—for the Laurents to be quite so... overtly aggressive."

"You think?" I asked, beginning to run out of patience. "*I* never mistook Melchior and his friends for nice friendly unassuming cuddly people, I have to say."

Marc nodded his head, slightly rueful. "They had their moments."

I bristled quietly, in no mood to lament about any vampire. Marc, sensitive as ever to those around him reached out a hand to take mine. "All I'm saying, is that I find it slightly surprising." He thought for a moment then added, "But fortunately you managed to take care of them?"

I grimaced. "Well... yes... Gwyn did. With the help of Mr Hoo. Do you remember him? My owl."

Kat nodded. "So cute."

"Not tonight he wasn't. He was a beast. I've never seen him like that. All claws and talons." I puffed out my cheeks and angled my fingers into claws. "But I was glad of his assistance."

"Maybe it was just a particularly vicious strain of bats that wanted to nest in the roof?" Kat suggested.

I thought back over the whole event. "Believe me, I wish that was the case." I shook my head reluctantly. "There was a thing—"

My companions stared at me, waiting for me to go on. "Definitely half bat, half... human form."

Marc nodded and his lip curled up. "It was dispatched?"

I let a noisy breath out. "Yes. It crumbled to dust as I watched."

Marc slumped in his chair. "I guess that's all the evidence we need."

Kat's face turned pale and she clutched at Marc's arm. "But we thought we would be safe here. That's why we came. What have we done?"

"You've walked into a trap," I said. "And now I'll have to find a way to get you out."

CHAPTER SIX

We spent the next day holed up in the inn. While Marc and Kat hid out in the darkest room in the attic, I tried to contact Wizard Shadowmender through the orb but he could not be reached. In the end I resorted to using the ancient Bakelite telephone we housed at the inn to call Mr Kephisto. He offered to come over and keep us company, but I didn't feel there was much point. I did ask him if he would have a go at reaching Wizard Shadowmender on our behalf though.

Gwyn and I hung out in the kitchen where it was warm. Florence was in and out, busily thinking up ideas for her book I assumed. I drank more tea than was good for me, and in spite of looking hopeful every time my housekeeper appeared, Florence failed to take the hint. Her frequent forays into the pantry yielded only individual ingredients she might utilise in one of her ingenious creations, but no actual cake for me to eat. I huffed moodily and gave Millicent a call.

Fortunately Millicent could be reached more easily than the elderly wizards, and upon hearing the headlines about the fracas from the previous evening she rushed up the lane to see me, leaving her dogs—Jasper was none too fond of vampires and we weren't sure about Sunny—at home.

"Oh my," she exclaimed when she saw my face. "You look like you've been trampled by a herd of cows."

"Bats," Gwyn told her, a word my great-grandmother was employing with startling regularity, but which was rapidly becoming my least favourite in the dictionary.

Millicent tilted my head to the light to get a better look at my eye. "That's nasty. Bats can carry rabies, you know?"

"Don't remind me," I grumbled.

She tsk-ed and tutted and parted my hair so that she could examine my scalp. "Some deep scratches here too."

"Do you have anything that can help?" I asked, my voice plaintive and needy.

"Poor Alf." Millicent smiled, understanding

immediately than I needed a mother's love. "Let me see what I can do for you."

She poked around in her potions bag and drew out several bottles, then began to mix a few drops of this and a couple of drops of that into a small mixing bowl. She carefully decanted the mix into a small bottle and gave it a good shake.

"What is that?" I asked as she poured a suspicious looking magenta liquid onto a wad of cotton wool.

"Tincture of iodine, white willow bark and a couple of teaspoons or turmeric oil."

"Okay," I said and relaxed a little as she began to dab at the wounds on my scalp.

"Laced with a little bromethalin and a crushed grain's worth of phosphorus."

I jerked away from her in alarm. "What?"

"Sshhh. You just have to trust me. You do trust me, don't you, Alf?"

"Isn't bromethalin what they use in rat poison?" I protested.

Millicent poked me. "You make such a fuss. Do you want to die of bat poisoning?"

Was that a possibility? No. I didn't. So I gave in to her ministering, all the while my mind cogitating on whether you should *ever* trust *anyone* that asked you to trust them.

"There, I think that takes care of your scalp." Millicent stood back to admire her handiwork. "I should perhaps have warned you that it might turn your hair green in places."

"Are you serious?" I asked, my voice two octaves higher than normal.

"Don't worry, Miss Alf," Florence floated into the room, a pile of notebooks and pens trailing in her wake. "Remember when Miss Charity had green hair. I believe the expression you used was that she 'rocked' that look."

"But that was Charity," I reminded my housekeeper. "She rocks all of her hairstyles because she has the sort of hair and the sort of face that... enable her to do that. Meanwhile, I've been afflicted with wild red hair, and you know what they say."

"Red and green should never be seen," Gwyn chipped in archly.

I wrinkled my nose at my great-grandmother. "Exactly."

Gwyn smirked. "What about her eye, Millicent? Do you think you'll be able to save her sight?" I did a double take. My eye wasn't that bad was it?

"What do you mean?" I wailed. "What aren't you telling me?"

Florence giggled. "I never knew you were such a baby, Miss Alf. I think they're pulling your leg."

Kat and Marc were able to join Finbarr and myself for supper once night had fallen. I'd persuaded Florence to cook a vegan vegetable and bean hotpot with lots of herbs from Gwyn's herb garden that would suit Marc. But although it looked and tasted wonderful, with the exception of Finbarr, we were all a little downhearted and listless. The Irish witch attacked the hot pot with gusto. For a little fellow, he sure could eat a lot.

Inspecting myself in the back of a serving spoon I reached the conclusion that I looked a tad more human. My hair *had* turned green in places, but I'd been in the shower and gently soaked out the rest of Millicent's tincture. She'd headed home but left me with a couple of ointments. She told me that the one for my eye had been concocted from witch hazel, calendula and mallow—but let's face it, it probably contained the viscous liquid drained from a one-eyed demon. There was also some 'TCP' for the cuts on my hands.

But that bottle *was* actually labelled TCP and had a price sticker from Whittle Stores on it, so I gave her the benefit of the doubt.

At dinner, I'd placed the orb on the kitchen table next to me, still waiting for Wizard Shadowmender to get in touch, but so far he was still AWOL. I mused on his silence.

"What about if we just jump back in the Volkswagen and turn around and go back where we came from?" Kat was asking. She was twitchy and with good reason.

Marc shook his head. "We can't, my love."

"They've flushed you out now. They'll be watching the inn to be sure," Finbarr added, scooping another ladleful of hot pot onto his plate.

I agreed with him. "We managed to avoid them knowing where you were for so long. We can't risk them following you from here to your safe house." I could have kicked the pair of them for being daft enough not to double check that the invitation to the inn had been genuine. What had they been thinking?

"When do you think they'll make another move?" Kat asked.

Finbarr and I looked at each other. "Don't you be worrying your little self about that now." Finbarr smiled at Kat to reassure her. "They can't be getting in here. It's locked up tighter than—"

"Yes, quite." I interrupted Finbarr, not quite sure where he was going with his analogy. He returned to shovelling food into his mouth quite happily. Fortunately his pixies were nowhere in sight but no doubt they'd be around to polish off whatever dinner was left over.

"Perhaps they won't come. They made a play and failed after all." Marc, ever the optimist, threw his arm around Kat.

"Mmm," I agreed doubtfully. Secretly I figured the vampires had begun testing the water and were now waiting to see what we could come after them with.

Marc smiled my way. "But... you know... Sabien and I... and Melchior... we go back a long way. I'm sure I could talk sense into them. Everything will be fine."

"I think you're missing the point here," I said, as politely as I was able. Marc just didn't appear to understand how much danger we were all in and yet he should have known, after all he'd lived among that twisted nest for a long time. I pointed at my swollen eye. "This wasn't inflicted by someone ready to talk sense. If it hadn't been for Mr Hoo, the bat would have tried to burrow into my brain."

"Alfhild," Gwyn interrupted me. When I looked her way she gently shook her head, discouraging me from scaring Kat and Marc unnecessarily. She was right. What we didn't need were the pair of them trying to bolt away in the middle of the night. We'd end up with a massacre on our hands one way or the other.

Darn it. What was keeping Wizard Shadowmender from returning my call?

"You would think Melchior would have got over himself by now," Kat ruminated, as she stroked Marc's hands. Seriously, those two never seemed to stop touching each other. "I think I was not such a good prize for him, you know? Not the one for him. He always had so many girlfriends that I imagined he would find somebody new quite quickly."

"Or hook up with one of the old ones, certainly," Marc agreed.

"I expect he has." They were right. Melchior wasn't one for letting the grass grow under his feet. He would have moved on. "But the thing is... just because he's taken up with some other poor woman won't mean he's forgiven you, will it? And besides—"

I glanced at Gwyn in case she wanted me to remain schtum. "I have a nasty feeling this is actually more to do with the death of Thaddeus."

"Thaddeus?" Marc repeated. "My goodness. I'd forgotten about him. Yes, of course. Poor Thaddeus."

How could he have forgotten? The memory of that sunny morning when Charity had flung open the curtain and Thaddeus, chained to his seat in the bar, had burned to a crisp had been indelibly scored onto my retina. I shivered.

"Tell me what you knew about him," I asked, curious as to what Marc would say.

Marc shrugged. "Thaddeus Corinthian. Turned when he was twenty-five or so. Lived in Paris near Sabien. He also had a beautiful chateau near Reims somewhere, but I think his family were from Transylvania originally. At least that's where the family seat is."

"There's a family seat?" That sounded rather impressive.

"I don't know the ins and outs," Marc replied. "He used to joke that he was a Prince, but you know with all the historical complexity that is the Transylvanian region, he may have been making that up." He shrugged. "He had an awful lot of money though—as most vampires seem to. I visited his apartment in

Paris, and he had a genuine Van Gogh on the wall of his lavatory. He found that funny."

"Hilarious." I thought for a moment, wondering if Gwyn would object to me re-hanging her rather severe looking portrait in one of the guest lavatories. "So who killed him?"

Marc shook his head slowly, his eyes wide. "We all thought you guys did."

"We?" I prompted.

"Yeah. Like… that's what Melchior and Sabien and Gorka were saying."

"It wasn't us," I said, my voice firm.

"Alfhild?" Gwyn, standing by the window and looking outside, called to me.

My nerves twanged. What had she seen? I didn't want to go out there again tonight for another showdown with a bunch of killer-bats. Finbarr was on his feet immediately, the remainder of the hotpot forgotten. He and I crowded into the bay window and peered out.

The bats were back, circling the house; evidently, they'd invited their friends. There were far more of them out there than the previous night.

From behind me came a sharp intake of breath. Kat, both hands to her mouth, looked about ready to scream the place down.

"They're not getting in here," I reassured her, and squeezed her arm. "Come on Kat. You're made of sterner stuff than this." Her eyes filled with tears at my words, and I wondered where that strong stoic woman I'd known twelve months ago had disappeared to.

"You don't understand," she whispered and looked at Marc, her eyes beseeching him.

He shrugged and looked a little bashful. "We're having a baby," he explained.

"You are?" I laughed in surprise. "But that's wonderful! I didn't know that was possible—" I thought twice about continuing that line of conversation and simply threw my arms around Kat. "I'm very happy for you!"

"As am I," Gwyn nodded. "But I can see why you're so concerned. We have to make sure you're safe."

Finbarr planted a kiss on Kat's cheek and shook Marc's hand. "The house is secure. You have my word on that," Finbarr told her.

I took a few steps towards the door, but Kat clutched at my arm. "You're not going out there are you?"

I shook my head and glanced at Finbarr because I couldn't speak for him or what he proposed to do.

"The perimeter in the woods is fine. I'm happy to stay in tonight," he confirmed.

"Grandmama?" I asked. "Are you intending to go out there and blast them out of the sky again?"

Gwyn pursed her lips. "No, my dear. I think I've had my fill of those ghastly creatures too. I'll head up to the attic and keep an eye on what is happening in the roof."

She began to fade. "Keep trying Wizard Shadowmender. It's not like him to be so remiss at getting back to people. I'm beginning to wonder whether something has happened to him."

"I will," I called after her.

Finbarr nodded. "I'm going to patrol the inn tonight, so you folks don't need to worry." He directed a quick knowing look my way. "I'll free the pixies, Alf. If that's okay?"

Under the circumstances what could I say? I nodded. "Alright. Just shout if you need any help."

"You get some rest," he said.

As he exited the bar I stole another quick glance outside. A large dark shape flew past the window, startling me, but it was only Mr Hoo soaring gracefully around, circling the lawn, disrupting the bats as they tried to pelt the roof of the inn. As I watched, worrying for his safety, I spotted another three owls flying towards the inn evidently intending to join him.

The bats had invited their friends.

So Mr Hoo had too.

And I never knew he had any!

I couldn't sleep.

Not surprising really. The orb sat quietly on my bedside table, Wizard Shadowmender not returning any of my calls. Mr Hoo was still hard at it outside, scattering bats left, right and centre. I heard him and his feathery friends calling to each other from time to time even through my closed window.

It actually sounded as though they were having a blast.

With Gwyn in the attic and Mr Hoo outside, I found myself sitting up in bed and feeling a little lonely. Marc and Kat had retreated to their attic bedroom, and although I occasionally heard light footsteps outside my door as Finbarr walked past, I felt oddly isolated. My thoughts turned to Silvan.

"I wish you were here," I whispered into the darkness. I could imagine how he would look at me if he could hear me. He would arch an eyebrow and smile at me with that smug knowing grin of his. "It's not because I like you," I hurriedly added. "Not at all. It's just because you would know what to do. How to fight off this threat."

I lay down and blinked at the ceiling, remembering all the times he had been there for me. His reassuring strength, his soft voice as he comforted me or issued instructions. The way he scolded me when I didn't have my wand at the ready, or I held on to too much tension and hadn't softened my knees when I began an attack. *You can't make good magick when you're tense*, he'd stated time and time again.

"I'm really tense now," I told him. Not that he could hear or would even appreciate the predicament I now found myself in. "I don't know what it is about vampires. They really give me the heebie-jeebies."

Let them go for now. His voice drifted out of the darkness. *You'll be no good to anyone if you don't get some sleep.*

"Are you here?" I asked as my body grew heavy.

I'm always with you.

I awoke just over four hours later. It had gone three

in the morning. I lay still, feeling peaceful and warm, considering a visit to the bathroom, wondering why I was awake. The inn was quiet.

Too quiet perhaps.

I couldn't hear Mr Hoo or his buddies. It might not mean anything untoward, but it was worth checking.

Reluctantly I extricated myself from the bedclothes and padded over to the window. There wasn't a huge amount of light out there given the cloud cover. I couldn't spot any bats either.

"Good work guys," I said assuming the owls had seen the critters off.

A glint to my left alerted me to something travelling up the lane towards the end of the drive. Headlights? A car?

I squinted into the distance. The progress of the light was slow. That was a good thing. There were potholes in the lane that could ruin your suspension and disable your axles if you weren't careful.

My inner witch twitch began to pulse.

"It's a car. Someone who has taken a wrong turning," I said out loud as if saying it would make it so.

Except of course it didn't make it so.

The light was blue.

And it bobbed as it advanced.

I knew exactly what it was.

"No," I cried. "No, no, no, no, no."

I turned about in panic but then spun back to the window again, making myself giddy. Maybe I'd imagined it.

I hadn't. "No!"

There was nothing for it but to head downstairs and ward off this latest unwelcome visitor. Grabbing my dressing gown and stuffing my feet into slippers, not easy when you're moving, I raced for the stairs.

Finbarr had obviously heard the commotion I'd been making or had also seen the light travelling down the lane, because he joined me on the front step of the inn just as I finished knotting my dressing gown cord.

He closed the door behind us to prevent access—or exit—from anyone or anything else and together we watched the slow procession of a single horse-drawn hearse. Unlike the previous visit from the vampire clan that Whittle Inn had 'enjoyed'—when there had been a dozen carriages, a dozen hearses, each pulled by six blinkered black horses wearing tall plumes of shiny black feathers—this was a solitary procession and yet still extraordinarily eerie.

The horses moved slowly, the wheels of the carriage spitting gravel as they trotted onto the drive. The masked driver pulled on the reins and the horses halted in front of us.

The driver stepped down as the horses whinnied and shook their heads, their harnesses jangling. The sound carried in the still night. I glanced around, pondering where Mr Hoo and his friends were and spotted a pair of gold eyes glinting at me from an oak tree on the edge of the drive. A single coachman alighted from the rear of the vehicle where he'd been clinging to the footplate. He began to untie leather straps, ready to free the coffin within the glass carriage.

"Whoa, hold your horses there, partner." I jumped off the step to confront him, but the driver moved in front of me and blocked access.

"Do you mind?" I glared at him. "This is private property and neither you nor your cargo are welcome here."

The driver stood a good ten inches taller than me and was probably twice as broad. I found his sheer physical size intimidating. Even working together with Finbarr—shorter and skinnier than me—we would struggle to make a dent in this guy's armour. Unless we used magick of course.

But I, as usual, had forgotten to pick up my wand. It remained in place, lying uselessly next to my mute communication orb.

The driver, staring down at me with dead eyes, reached inside his long wool cloak and pulled out an envelope. Red ink on nauseatingly familiar parchment.

My repulsion overrode my nerves and my fingers were surprisingly steady as I ripped the envelope open.

Ms Daemonne

Forgive this unexpected intrusion. Recent events have meant it is imperative that I visit with you at Whittle Inn.

You may have every confidence that you and your friends are safe. At least from me.

I travel alone.

Please stow my coffin safely and I will attend you tomorrow after dark.

In the meantime, in the interests of your continued wellbeing, accept no other visitors. None.

Your obedient servant

Sabien Laurent

Chapter Seven

And that's how it was that Finbarr, Gwyn and I came to be sitting in the bar just before eight the following evening. Gwyn floated restlessly backwards and forwards, creating a draft that made me shiver. Her hatred of vampires unnerved me. She was a ghost and one of the best witches I knew. Why would a vampire scare her?

I watched her uneasily. What could I do? The orb lay on the table, inert and useless. All attempts to contact Wizard Shadowmender had failed. I hadn't even been able to call Mr Kephisto or Penelope Quigwell because I couldn't get a signal on my mobile. The inn's broadband was down—not an unusual occurrence, given the rubbish coverage in my part of East Devon—and even the Bakelite telephone wouldn't connect to the Paranormal Telephone Company switchboard.

Something, somewhere, was really wrong.

I'd insisted that Kat and Marc remained hidden in the attic well out of the way of Sabien. Unsurprisingly, they'd agreed. Kat's usually beautiful face appeared worn now, and I regretted the amount of upset I had caused her by accepting Sabien's plea for sanctuary at the inn.

For now, I could only hope against hope that he would deliver his message and then leave again tonight.

At eight precisely a noise alerted us from the back hall. He used the external steps from the beer cellar to enter through the back door.

We turned expectantly as he pushed open the glass door to the bar. He was much as I remembered from his previous visit. Tall at six feet (not as tall as his driver) and with well-coiffed silver hair that had once been dark. He dressed with care; an immaculate Italian suit in soft charcoal wool, an expensive shirt and a silk cravat in maroon. Gold cufflinks, a solid gold watch and a chunky signet ring completed his look. His eyes were inky, bottomless black wells of death you could lose your soul in.

I had no intention of ever doing that.

"Ms Daemonne."

Yes, I remembered that luscious French accent of his.

He bowed slightly and reached for my hand. I refused to extend it. Ungracious on my part, but a witch has to have certain standards. I remembered the papery feel of his lips on my knuckles from before and I shuddered in revulsion.

Without acknowledging the slight, he stood straight and drew his heels together. He dressed like a gentleman and behaved like an officer. "I apologise for calling on you in this manner. Believe me, eet eez as difficult for me as eet eez for you."

"If you don't want to be here, perhaps you should have saved yourself the trip." My words were as cold as my heart.

"You 'ave not heard from Weezard Shadowmender, I take eet?"

I chewed on the inside of my cheek. How did he know? *What* did he know?

When I refrained from answering, he nodded. "That eez what I expected and why I 'ad to come 'ere."

He looked longingly at the optics behind the bar. "I don't suppose I could wet my wheestle? Just a leetle?"

Reluctantly I relented and unbent myself

enough to go and pour him a drink. I couldn't recall what his tipple had been before—the goddess knew we'd gone through far more red wine than was healthy while his nest had been staying at the inn—so I poured him a large glass of *Courvoisier*.

He took it from me with a smile of thanks and drank half of it in one gulp. "That eez so good. You should have one too. Help you relax a leetle."

"I'm relaxed enough," I snapped, but he was right. I poured a small snifter for myself and one for Finbarr although I knew my Irish witch friend would have preferred whisky.

I took a sip of my drink and the brandy slipped down my throat, warming me through. I peered at Sabien over the top of my glass. "Do you want to explain what is going on?"

"*Sláinte*." Finbarr lifted his drink in salute and downed it in one. I pushed the bottle over to him so he could refill his glass. He smiled impishly.

"Grave news, Alfhild," Sabien offered without any further hesitation.

"I'm afraid that you are struggling to communicate with your leaders precisely because that is what the *Vampiri* want. Zey are choosing to block your communications."

"The...? What?" I glanced at Gwynn and back at Sabien.

"*Vampiri*. The Romanian arm of the Vampire Nation."

"They've blocked communication?" Gwyn floated into place alongside me. "How have they done this?"

Sabien shook his head. "*Je ne sais pas*. But zey somehow have zis power."

"Rubbish," I said. I'd never heard of *Vampiri*.

Sabien gestured at me with his glass. "Not so, Ms Daemonne. These are not creatures to be dismissed lightly, I can assure you. They are powerful, more powerful than you can eemagine. And regretfully, zey 'ave decided ah... I don't know 'ow to say theese... *faire la guerre aux sorcières*."

Gwyn spun on him in shock, her wand levelled at him, and I swear if she'd been a wolf her hackles would have been standing on end.

"Grandmama?" I asked in alarm. "What did he say?"

Gwyn glared at Sabien with a hatred that would have made any other creature wither. "This impertinent piece of bat scat thinks to intimidate us," she spat. "He claims his *Vampiri* imagine they can wage war on witches."

"War?" I recoiled from Sabien in horror. "You can't be serious?"

"Deadly." Sabien's black eyes stared into the bottom of his brandy glass. I couldn't interpret his feelings. His passivity made it difficult for me to work out what his angle was on all this. I didn't even know whether we were safe inside the inn within his presence.

I shifted uncomfortably and exchanged a meaningful look with Finbarr. My own hand crept towards the pocket where my wand nestled. Gwyn still pointed hers at the vampire, the expression on her face unequivocal. She would happily destroy him with a Curse of Madb or whatever it took if he so much as dared to breathe out of time.

Finbarr waved his glass at Sabien and effected an incredulous laugh. "How do they intend to achieve this war on witches? To be sure, witches outnumber vampires across the world probably four or five to one."

The corners of Sabien's mouth twitched. "You British witches 'ave such an inflated sense of self. You think ze rest of ze world owes you a favour. That every witch who walks ze earth will come to your rescue. This eez not the case."

"I'm not British; I'm Irish," Finbarr corrected

him. "But I'll stand with my brothers and sisters here I can assure you."

"You are brave *mon ami*, and possibly very stupid."

The lights in the bar flickered. Once, twice. Then they went out altogether.

My wand was in my hand instantly, even as my breath caught in my throat. I reached out with all my senses searching for a threat. The fingers of energy that rushed from me tripped and tangled with Finbarr's and Gwyn's... each of us searching for danger... then freed themselves and moved on, spreading ever outwards.

Gwyn lit the tip of her wand, illuminating the room.

At the extremities of what I could see, my ghosts flittered around us. Gradually more light threaded down the hallway as Florence and Zephaniah brought the half-a-dozen lit candles we kept under the sink for emergencies. They set them up around the bar, bathing us in warm light once more.

In all this time Sabien stood stock still, nursing his brandy. He appeared neither alarmed nor supercilious. He merely watched as events unfolded around him.

"Why would you choose to warn us?" I asked the

obvious question. "Why are you even here? Why not simply attack us and have done with it?"

He looked at me, but his face remained expressionless. "Because zis whole thing started 'ere. At Whittle Inn."

"When Thaddeus was killed," I confirmed. I'd been right.

Sabien nodded.

"But why war?" Finbarr asked, sounding as confused as I felt. His eyes flicked around the room, scrutinizing the shadows, searching for hidden dangers.

"Why so extreme," I demanded. "A war by all vampires on all witches? Think of the implications! That could break out of our small communities and overspill. It would inevitably end up involving ordinary mortals. It would devastate the world!"

"That's what these monsters want." Gwyn directed her vitriol at Sabien. "That's what they've always wanted; an end to witches. Then they'll be able to feed where they want and when they want. There'll be no stopping them."

"I must admit zat would be an entertaining proposition," Sabien said but without humour.

"You said that not all witches would come to our

rescue," I remembered. "What did you mean by that?"

Sabien locked eyes with me. "I really cannot tell you."

My mind raced. Was he suggesting that there were witches in league with the *Vampiri*? It wouldn't be unknown for certain bands of warlocks to join forces with vampires as long as the deal brokered was mutually beneficial.

The blood ran cold in my veins. There had to be more to this than met the eye.

I asked again. "Why did you come, Sabien? What is it you want?"

This time the elegant vampire smiled. He reached out and took the *Courvoisier* bottle from Finbarr and poured himself another healthy measure.

"I have been charged with sending you to Castle Iadului."

"Castle Yadolooie?"

"Iadului."

"Yadaloy? Where is that?"

"It's the seat of the Corinthians." A voice drifted out of the shadows and I watched as Sabien's eyes lit up. Marc stepped forwards. "That's where Thaddeus came from, and where his father still lives."

"Bonsoir Marc," Sabien smiled, unsheathing his teeth.

"Sabien," Marc replied pleasantly enough.

"You want me to go to Transylvania?" I sought clarification.

"If eet ees not too much trouble." Sabien nodded.

Marc shook his head. "You most certainly can't go, Alf. It would be like walking into a den of vipers."

"Well there you have it," I told Sabien. I didn't have a burning desire to meet Thaddeus's father, that was for sure.

"I'm afraid eet eez completely out of your 'ands now, Ms Daemonne." Sabien grinned at me across the top of his glass, the burnished liquid sparkling brilliantly in the candlelight. "You are a diplomatic tool. A chess piece if you will. A pawn."

I shifted uneasily. He couldn't make me go to Transylvania against my will.

Sabien lifted his glass towards the ceiling, and as if by magick—and as far as I knew Sabien couldn't perform any kind of magick—the lights came back on, glowing steadily and dispelling the shadows. From upstairs came the sound of the familiar hard ring and thumping vibration of the Bakelite telephone on my desk. In my pocket my mobile began to trill.

At the same time my orb, until now lying idle on the bar, burst into brilliant life. It sparkled and glowed, rapidly changing colour, a kaleidoscope of rainbow hues, that spun and shimmied as though I were about to receive dozens of different messages from many different people.

Sabien watched me as I cautiously reached for the orb, a small smile playing at the corner of his lips. Somehow the communication block had been lifted. Was it true what he had said then? Could the *Vampiri* control our communication systems?

As the clouds parted and Wizard Shadowmender's concerned face appeared beneath the glass, my stomach sank.

I was about to find out just how much trouble I was in.

Chapter Eight

They sent a sleek black BMW for me. I stared out of the window at the dark horizon and occasional blinking lights as we cruised through the night. Eventually, the car pulled up in an unusually quiet Celestial Street. Many businesses tended to remain open even overnight here, seeking to accommodate those witches who prefer the hours of darkness to go about their business. But in this final hour before dawn, even the night owls had forsaken their need to shop.

The grand building that housed the Council of Witches might have been mistaken for a town hall by those who didn't know otherwise. Centuries old, from the front it looked like any other Greco-Roman mausoleum to municipal bureaucracy, but behind the sturdy doors lay the most hallowed chambers known to my kind.

I'd only been here once before. This is where I'd had to register the death of my mother Yasmin. That seemed like a lifetime ago now, but it had been the event, just eighteen months before, that had set me on my current path.

I climbed out of the car and immediately found myself surrounded by burly security guards. They swept me away from Sabien and into the massive reception hall with its gilt columns and Renaissance murals. I followed mutely as they led me down a series of marble staircases, our footsteps echoing around the stairwells.

We moved into a plainer hallway and began to navigate a series of security doors. Each of these had to be opened with a palm print, and the final three required a retinal scan too. Finally at the end of a particularly long corridor, I was shunted through a plain door into a busy office.

I gazed around with eyes as wide as saucers. I imagined that the control room at NASA looked something like this. But with a different type of personnel perhaps. Here, witches and wizards worked away at desks, staring at computer screens and tapping away at keyboards. Others chatted into headsets. I thought I could hear people speaking in French and German and another in what might have been Chinese or something similar. On the walls were numerous screens with maps of the world, and maps of the galaxy. Across these, little lights were moving around, being monitored. One or two wizards gazed up at one particular screen, frowning as a colleague traced her finger over the outline of something. "That can't be right," she was saying.

"We need to report this," agreed the other.

People moved around with a sense of urgency and efficiency. I didn't quite know where to put myself. While I waited to be told what to do next or where to go, my only relief was that I'd finally been separated from Sabien.

"Oh hi, Alf." A familiar soft voice caught my attention and I swivelled to the left in surprise.

"Ross! Hi!" Ross Baines was a ghost I'd 'recruited' on the railway tracks at Canary Wharf. A technical wizard he now worked with Penelope Quigwell. He was one of the sweetest young men I knew; always mild-mannered and unfailingly polite. He was a whizz at what he did, and I had a feeling he had stolen Florence's heart.

Not that she would have admitted that of course.

"What are you doing here?" Ross asked me. "You look a little peaky if you don't mind me saying so."

"I feel a little peaky," I said. "I've received a summons."

"An invitation you couldn't refuse, eh?" Ross winced in sympathy. "Everything has kicked off here. They're talking about going to war."

I nodded; my misery complete. "That's why I'm here."

"Oh dear."

A door at the end of the room opened and Penelope bustled out. Spotting me she waved us over. The security guard gave me a little push.

"There's absolutely no need for that," Ross told him. "Ms Daemonne is a friend of mine, so kindly take it easy, sir!"

I smiled, grateful for his small expression of kindness. I waved my fingers at him as I headed for where Penelope waited.

"Come through," Penelope ordered me. I didn't expect any consideration from her. She'd always been a cold fish.

I stepped through the door. A large desk, with several computer screens and keyboards set up on it, dominated the room. Penelope had obviously been beavering away at something. On this side of the desk were several chairs. Wizard Shadowmender and another gentleman were standing, evidently waiting for my arrival.

"Ah, Alfhild," Wizard Shadowmender said. "So good of you to join us." *As though I'd had any sort of say in the matter at all.* "May I introduce you to Ambassador Rubenscarfe?"

The gentleman, a wizard I guessed, wore a smart dark navy suit with a pale blue tie in lieu of robes. He had a receding hairline, a neatly clipped beard and moustache, all in pale brown fading to salt and pepper. He had a pair of John Lennon spectacles perched on the end of his nose, and now he regarded me through them with evident curiosity. After a couple of beats, he held out his hand.

"So this is Alfhild Daemonne," he said.

I shook his hand, on automatic pilot. "Pleased to meet you."

"You've been causing trouble, I hear?" The Ambassador quipped.

I opened my mouth to retort but from the corner of my eye spotted Wizard Shadowmender shaking his head and rolling his eyes.

"Take a seat, Alf," Wizard Shadowmender directed me. "Would you like some tea?"

"Might I have a coffee, please? I haven't managed

any sleep." I tried not to glower, but seriously, I was beginning to lose my marbles.

"I'll see to it." Penelope left the room.

"Alf," my elderly wizard friend announced as he took a seat behind the desk. "We're in a spot of bother."

"A spot, you say?" interjected the Ambassador. "The *Vampiri* are declaring war on us following a diplomatic incident at this young woman's hostelry. They claim the entire Vampire Nation are behind them. That's hardly a spot of bother, is it?"

"A diplomatic incident?" I repeated. "Is that how this is being escalated?"

"It really doesn't need much escalation," the Ambassador retorted. "You've seen to that yourself."

This was patently unfair, and I had no intention of letting him get away with saying such a thing. "Thaddeus Corinthian was killed at my inn nearly twelve months ago. I didn't see a great deal of interest from anyone back then. Not the Ministry of Witches nor this *Vampiri* group, let alone The Vampire Nation."

"Unfortunately it appears that his father, Prince Grigor Corinthian of Wallachia, has taken extreme umbrage," Wizard Shadowmender told me gruffly.

"It would appear that he wants to use it as an excuse to hit back at us."

"But why now?" I asked. "After all this time?"

"We're not sure," Wizard Shadowmender admitted, "and that's why we are going to acquiesce to the Prince's request that you fly out to Transylvania and meet him at Castle Iadului."

"But... but..." I recoiled from the memory of Marc telling me they were a nest of vipers.

"Consider it a diplomatic mission." The Ambassador smiled the toothy grin of a hungry alligator.

I sighed deeply, frustrated by the man's apparent stupidity. "I really don't think that's a good idea. No good can ever come from mixing with these people."

Penelope picked that moment to return with a mug of decent-smelling coffee and a plate of biscuits. She placed them on the desk in front of me and clicked a button on her keyboard. A screen on the wall lit up.

"We've found her. She's connected." Penelope nodded at Wizard Shadowmender and he directed my attention to the screen.

"We assumed you wouldn't be too keen, Alf."

"Merry meet, Alfhild."

I turned to stare at the screen in shock. An old woman, much older than Wizard Shadowmender, peered out at me. I recognised her instantly. It hadn't been many weeks since I'd last been in her presence. Neamh, Mother of Witches. The most divine of the living goddesses. She had long silver hair that luminesced with life; her dark, aged skin glowed with ruddy health. Among witches there was no superior authority than she, and to be in her charismatic presence was a great honour.

"Mother." I bowed my head in respect, unwilling to meet her bright gaze, half afraid she would strike me down for causing so much trouble at Whittle Inn. "I can explain," I said, continuing to look at the floor.

"Alfhild," she said again, and the word was a command. Reluctantly I stole a look at her. I could see slight concern in the crease of her brow, but in her eyes, there was only love.

"We're in a bit of a pickle," she said. Her choice of words surprised me—in a good way.

"I'm sorry—" I began to apologise but she waved my words away, a fiery glint in her eyes.

"Oh tosh! The Transylvanian *Vampiri* are out to make trouble, and The Vampire Nation are evidently keen to back them at the moment, but let's just to see how far it gets them. They've latched onto the most convenient excuse they can find. Unfortunately that does place us in a bit of a bind at this time. Don't you agree, Wizard Shadowmender?"

"Oh I do, Mother Neamh. Most definitely." Wizard Shadowmender winked at me.

"Penelope?" Neamh enquired.

Penelope came out from behind the desk to stand beside me so that she could be seen. She carried a clipboard containing a few printouts and a pen in her hand. "I'm in agreement too, Mother Neamh." She brandished her notes. "If I may?"

"Of course." The old witch in the screen leaned closer to whatever was being used to relay her image as though she would be able to read the details over Penelope's shoulder.

"Grigor Corinthian comes from an illustrious and renowned vampire family. In fact they claim a blood-line with the notorious Vlad Țepeș—although that's not something we have been able to verify. Nonetheless his line have been feted as princes for many centuries." She flipped over a page. "It seems Grigor was born in 1734 to Prince Petr Corinthian and an unknown mother. You know how it is with their kind?" Penelope sniffed. "Grigor has himself taken a number of wives, including Rose Alberta Moretti in 1841. She is a Princess of Italian descent and gave birth to Thaddeus while she was still a mortal, in

1864. There are rumours of two male siblings, one older, one younger but we haven't been able to find much out about either of them. We're still searching."

I wondered where all this was going.

"Our intelligence suggests that after the unfortunate death of Thaddeus at...," Penelope nodded at me, "... Alf's inn, there wasn't a huge amount of reaction, neither at Grigor's court or in Italy where Princess Rose Moretti now lives with her own small cadre. We see no evidence that suggests that Thaddeus was particularly close to anyone in his family. He had been living in Paris, sporadically between 1882 and 1914, but he travelled a great deal. He moved into an apartment on Saint-Germain-des-Prés in 1934 and has actually owned the building itself for many years."

I recognised the address. "Sabien—"

"Lives in the same building."

"Thaddeus was his landlord." That surprised me.

"The point is—" Penelope directed her words back to Neamh on the screen, "—Grigor Corinthian was not overly concerned about the death of Thaddeus at the time it occurred. He has many offspring from his harem of wives," Penelope uttered the words with complete distaste. "As you intimated Mother Neamh, the fact that he chooses to make a move against Alf now, and also rope in the assistance of The Vampire Nation is simply an excuse. It's probably something he's been looking at doing for months. He wants to stir up a hornet's nest amongst us witches."

A tap sounded against the door and Ross poked his head around. "We found this." A sheet of paper blew in and Penelope grabbed it. Ross winked at me and retreated. The door closed behind him while Penelope read the contents of his missive.

"Ah," Penelope said. "Fresh intelligence from our counterparts in the Ukraine. This might explain it."

"What does it say?" Mother Neamh asked.

"It appears that Grigor's eldest son, Mikhael we think, was last reported as domiciled in the USA. But he's has not been active for over six months."

"Destroyed?" Wizard Shadowmender asked.

Penelope shrugged. "Unconfirmed."

"So you're thinking that Grigor is suddenly worried that certain powers are destroying his heirs? That would make sense. Good work as always, Penelope." Penelope flushed a little pink and bowed to the Mother of Witches before stepping away and busying herself at her desk.

Where did that leave me?

"Alfhild." Mother Neamh turned her kind scrutiny back to me. "I'm sorry to drag you away from your inn but the threat was initially made to you and your guests. What we are hearing through various channels is that unless we turn you, Marc Williams and Ekaterina Lukova over to The Vampire Nation they will raise the stakes—so to speak—quite considerably."

"You can't be considering sending Marc and Kat to Transylvania," I blurted out in alarm, completely forgetting whom I was speaking to for a moment.

"Certainly not. I couldn't have that on my conscience."

I grimaced. The goddess alone knew what would happen to them and their baby if they were delivered into Melchior's keeping. It didn't bear thinking about.

"However, I am going to ask you to go, Alfhild."

I stepped backwards, a reflex flight reaction. My mouth dropped open in astonishment. "You... Me...? What?" I swallowed hard. There was silence in the room. "You want to turn me in to the Corinthians?"

She couldn't be serious. They'd rip me to pieces.

Limb from limb. Then scatter the pieces across Northern Europe.

"I'm not going to insist you go, of course." Neamh's gentle voice broke through my rising levels of panic. "And you won't be going alone."

I looked hopefully at Wizard Shadowmender. If I tagged along with him, everything would be alright.

"Ambassador Rubenscarfe will lead the diplomatic mission, and we will send a number of security personnel out with you."

My heart sank. I hadn't warmed to the Ambassador. Hopefully he knew his stuff.

"Why do you need me to go?" I asked.

"We're hoping you can help to soothe the ragged tempers," Mother Neamh smiled, "and maybe really get to the heart of what is going on out there. At the very least find out more about the youngest son."

I slumped in my aeroplane seat, staring out the window as the plane taxied along the runway heading for our final destination.

So this was Bucharest?

The sky, a forbidding slate grey, could have been my gaoler. I hadn't been able to escape coming here no matter how much I had protested, and once the Mother of Witches had become involved I'd had to zip it anyway.

They were hanging me out to dry.

Following assurances from both Sabien and Wizard Shadowmender that everyone at the inn would remain safe and unharmed, I'd been ordered to attend Wizard Shadowmender and the Council of Witches at their headquarters in Celestial Street, London. Sabien and I had travelled up together in a black limousine, neither of us making eye contact or deigning to converse with the other.

My emotions pummelled me, collided head on and left me breathless and confused. I confess I found myself both scared and more than a little furious.

How in the goddess's name had I ended up in this mess?

Thaddeus had died horribly, but not by my hand.

For some reason the Ambassador warranted a seat in first class while I had to make do with economy. The flight, just over three hours in duration, was devoid of snacks which added to my misery. Fortunately it passed without incident, save for the large Romanian chap in the seat next to me who fell asleep and dribbled on my shoulder.

I shouldn't have, but I couldn't help myself. I muttered a little 'zip-it-up' spell that glued his mouth together every time he fell asleep. Effectively that meant he could only breathe through his nose, which had the effect of waking him up with a jolt, at which point his mouth was freed from the hex.

We repeated this cycle ad nauseum throughout the short trip, but don't worry, I did remember to release him entirely from the spell before I uttered a cheery goodbye.

Night was falling by the time we arrived. This part of Central Europe was an hour ahead of UK time and in any case at this time of the year darkness came earlier and earlier. Not entirely unexpectedly Romania seemed several degrees cooler than London. I shivered as I stepped down onto the tarmac. A stretch black limousine waited to take me and Ambassador Rubenscarfe to Castle Iadului. The other plane passengers stared at us curiously as we were directed straight from the plane to the car. Of the security personnel I'd been promised back at the Ministry of Witches in Celestial Street, there was no sign.

I slid across the leather of the backseat so that I could stare out of the window as we began our journey. I hadn't travelled much in Europe and I was curious about the landscape. As we set off, it rapidly became obvious that there wouldn't be a huge amount to see. Once we were out of town, ramshackle buildings lined the route and then became few and far between. We drove North and slightly east for a hundred miles or so towards Brașov, climbing the Southern Carpathians, and then followed the route of the River Olt west for another few dozen kilometres until finally we arrived at Castle Iadului.

Our driver—a tall and broad man dressed in a dark suit who reminded me very much of the hearse drivers that had turned up at Whittle Inn but without a mask in this case and sporting sunglasses instead, which seemed ridiculous given how dark it was everywhere—remained mute for the entire journey. Ambassador Rubenscarfe occasionally deigned to glance up from his iPad to tell me where we were, but for the most part the journey of nearly three hours was passed in lonely silence.

This gave me plenty of time to ponder on the meaning of life and what exactly Neamh hoped to achieve by sending me into the lion's den. What was it she thought I could do that would help ease tensions between The Vampire Nation and ourselves?

For now I was stumped.

"Iadului." The driver spoke to us at last.

"Yadaloy." I repeated the unfamiliar sounding word as I leaned forward in my massive seat and gazed out at the front window to where he was pointing. For the past fifteen minutes we had been winding deeper and deeper through a dark pine forest, the headlights of the car picking up the startled faces of the occasional deer and very little else.

With my expectation based solely on vampire movies, Castle Iadului did not disappoint. Set high on a jagged hill, surrounded by rocks and boulders that fell away to the valley floor, the Castle towered high above everything surrounding it. I had a brief view of a huge medieval stone edifice, its narrow windows burning with yellow light, and then we were back among the trees and winding our way up a steep incline.

Up and up we went, until I imagined we must be among the clouds, for the mist came down and the driver slowed the car to take account of the deteriorating conditions. At one stage I looked out of my own window and the mist parted enough for me to see the extent of the drop to the valley below. My stomach lurched and I was mightily pleased I hadn't eaten anything properly for twenty-four hours. I sat back and buckled my seat belt. After that I didn't look out of that window again for a while.

Finally the car slowed to a standstill in front of a bridge. I craned my neck to look past the driver and observed a drawbridge slowly lowering into place. It didn't take long and then we were on our way again, the bridge clanging loudly as we trundled over it towards the entry of a thick outer wall.

I swivelled my head to look out the back and watched the drawbridge rise once more. We were trapped inside this castle unless there was another way out. My nerves clanged along with the sound of heavy iron meeting heavy iron. I didn't like this, one little bit.

The driver pulled up outside the main castle building. As we approached, a massive set of double doors at the top of a flight of stone steps swung open emitting a warm golden light. Someone unlocked my door and flung it wide. I stepped out into the cold night air, with knees that seemed to shake with exhaustion.

And maybe a little terror.

"Good evening, Ambassador Rubenscarfe. Good evening, Miss Daemonne." A woman with a thick

Eastern European accent, dressed in a dark business suit, greeted us. The milky paleness of her face, the blood red of her lipstick and empty black eyes identified her for what she was. "I am Nadia Cozma. I work for the *Vampiri* Diplomatic Service and I am charged with ensuring your stay is a pleasant one."

When she took my hand to shake it, her skin was as cold as ice. I shivered.

"Please," she said. "You must be tired. I will show you to your suite. No need to join us this evening. We will serve supper to your room."

"I would very much like to see Prince Grigor Corinthian this evening," Ambassador Rubenscarfe protested, but Nadia silenced him with the most frigid of smiles.

"That is entirely out of the question Ambassador. Prince Grigor is hunting tonight."

My stomach rolled in revulsion.

Nadia turned on her six-inch heels. Without looking back to check we were following she gracefully climbed the stone steps to the main entrance. After a long moment, where the Ambassador and I exchanged stricken glances, he followed her.

Swallowing hard, so did I.

They had some sort of electricity within Castle Iadului, that much was obvious; chandeliers burned brightly in the massive entrance hall lit, with hundreds of tiny lightbulbs rather than candles. We progressed up a grand central staircase—wide enough for a lorry—to the first floor, and then up a slightly less grand one to the second floor. Here the Ambassador and I, in spite of my protests, were split up. He was taken to the right by Nadia and I was led along a corridor to my left by a nameless man in another smart suit with eyes as black as coal.

At this point the grandeur of the floors below suddenly ended. We reached the corner staircase, and from then on, the floor and walls that wound their way up to the next few levels were carved from stone. Rather than electric lights, torches burning at strategic spots illuminated our route, meaning we were never quite out of the shadows. I expected the day-to-day residents of the castle liked it that way—vampire mood lighting, maybe?

I lost count of how many times I walked round and round, climbing up and up. My knees ached and my lungs burned. Fortunately I only had a small backpack with me, so I didn't have to lug a massive suitcase in my wake.

I'd decided we must be heading for the attic, so I

was pleasantly surprised when my black-eyed guide opened a small wooden door in the thick wall that led out into another long corridor. We walked past several closed doors on both sides, until he pushed open the third on the left with a flourish and stood back to allow me through.

I inched past him, straining to see inside. Nadia had called it a suite, but it looked nothing like the suites at Whittle Inn. For one, the room was high, maybe twelve or fourteen feet, and it was spacious too. An enormous four-poster bed, hung with thick tapestries, took centre stage. Huge tapestries also graced the walls, while a fire burned in an enormous stone grate as large as the one in the bar of my wonky inn. And this was only a bedroom... There was a sofa and a couple of easy chairs arranged around the fire, a small table set for dinner, and the stone floor had been covered by numerous antique silk Persian rugs.

"Is there a bathroom?" I turned to enquire politely of my guide, but he only stared at me blankly and then without further ado stepped backwards and closed the door.

"Maybe he doesn't speak much English," I said to the now empty room.

I heard the familiar clink and clunk of keys being turned in the locks. I dropped my bag and tracked back to the door, rattling it and then beating against the heavy wood. "Hey! Hey?" I called. "That's not part of the deal. Unlock this door!"

The sound of footsteps heading away on the stone floor outside told me that my demand had fallen on deaf ears. I turned about in despair.

"Oh no. No no no. This is not good," I chanted under my breath. "Why would they do that?" I rushed across the room to another wooden door I'd spotted. This opened easily enough but only into a bathroom. A massive iron claw-foot bath and an old-fashioned toilet with the cistern above your head filled the room, but there were no windows or other doors in this room.

Disconsolate, I headed back into the main bedroom. On either side of the fireplace a window, both intricate with stained glass, were locked. I rattled the handles willing something to budge. They didn't. I'd have to break them to get out. Given the number of stairs I'd climbed in order to get to the room, and how high I must be. I shuddered at the thought.

I stared around at the extravagantly decorated room, the comfortable bed, the tapestried walls and cheerful fire, and bit my lip.

I patted the wand in my pocket, reassured by its

presence. Of course I could unlock the doors using my magick, but that wouldn't explain why the vampires wanted to lock me in and hold me prisoner. It certainly wasn't the welcome I'd hoped for.

"Welcome to Castle Yadaloy," I said glumly.

CHAPTER NINE

I didn't so much sit on the sofa as perch.

The fire burned hot and bright, yet I struggled to get warm. I held the orb in one hand, having made several attempts to contact Wizard Shadowmender but to no avail thus far. I checked my mobile, but unsurprisingly, here in the back of the Transylvanian beyond, I wasn't getting much of a signal, and given what I knew about the way The Vampire Nation could block communication, I wasn't entirely surprised not to be able to use any of my devices.

My body felt tight with stress. My head ached. Hunger pangs created a swell of nausea. I rummaged in my bag for a mint or something—anything—but I found no witchy first aid kit to come to my rescue.

A clink by the door alerted me to a visitor. I sprang to my feet straight away, my wand drawn.

"No need for alarm," Nadia said, pushing the

door open and eyeing my wand. She stood back to allow a tall, broad man dressed in a black cloak and a black leather mask into the room. He took a quick look around and then nodded at Nadia. Nadia gestured into the hallway and another woman, this one bent double with age and dressed in clothes a peasant might have worn in a European fairy tale of old, entered my suite. The old dear didn't make eye contact with me, just shuffled to the table and set a tray down. When she began to empty the covered plates onto the table Nadia motioned her away with an air of irritability.

"Eat and sleep, Miss Daemonne. Tomorrow you will have your first audience with Prince Grigor Corinthian. Until then..." She bowed slightly and began to retreat from the room.

"Wait," I called, running after her. The guard stepped in front of Nadia, folding his thick forearms across his chest, blocking my way.

"There is nothing further to discuss at this time, Miss Daemonne," Nadia called back. The guard followed her out and firmly closed the door.

I banged on the wood, listening to the clink of keys and the clang of the locks. "You can't keep me prisoner here."

A quiet voice behind me almost made me jump

out of my skin. "Maybe you shouldn't think of it as a prison and more as protection, Madam."

I turned about in surprise. I couldn't see anyone.

"Hello?" I asked, frowning in suspicion.

"Perhaps you would do me the pleasure of acknowledging me, Madam?"

A ghost light. I hadn't spotted it before, preoccupied by my own thoughts as I had been. It hovered near one of the windows.

"Come to me," I told it, "be seen." I watched as the light, not much larger than a soccer ball, spun and elongated until it stood around five feet or so in height and rapidly gained colour and substance (well... after a fashion. It was a ghost after all). I found myself in the presence of a relatively short round man with a bald pate and a fine curly moustache. He displayed a proud military bearing and stood looking at me expectantly.

"Well this is terribly exciting," he said in native English. "It's a rather long time since anyone actually looked me in the eye."

"Is that so?" I asked, not experiencing any level of excitement myself, although I had to agree with him that the situation was terrible. "Who might you be? And what are you doing here?"

The gentleman bowed. "My name is Archibald

Peters. I'm a—I was a—Colonel in the 14th King's Regiment of Dragoons for many years."

"Which King would that be?" I enquired, requiring a little more context.

"Why King William IV, Madam. Who else?"

I nodded, wracking my brain to come up with a date and deciding he'd been alive sometime in the vicinity of the early nineteenth century. Perhaps. "What brought you here to Castle Yadoloy?"

"After my retirement from active service I became a trusted envoy of Her Imperial Majesty, Queen Victoria. I escorted a diplomatic mission here to the castle in 1846 and unfortunately I met my demise."

I scrutinised the ghost in front of me. "How did you... meet your end?" I asked. Experience with ghosts had taught me that this could be a delicate question at times; normally among those who didn't realise they were dead. The Colonel obviously understood exactly what had happened to him.

"I'm no medical professional, but I think my old ticker just decided to give out, Madam." He stood straight and stuck his chest out. "Appearances can be deceptive. I'm not a young man."

I held a smile in check. He was a gentleman in his sixties or early seventies perhaps. "Just one of those things then," I marvelled. Odd to find someone so quintessentially English in such a hideous place as this.

My head buzzed, suddenly giddy. I put an arm out to steady myself.

"If I may, Madam. You look a little peaky yourself." The Colonel appeared concerned. "Perhaps you should take a seat?"

"I'll be fine," I said automatically. The faint scent of food emanating from the table had my stomach rolling, but I knew that if I could only eat something I would feel a million times better. I pointed at the tray. "Would you mind if I ate while we carried on with our conversation?"

"No, by all means, Madam. Be my guest." The Colonel waited until I took my seat at the table and then joined me, hovering close by.

I lifted a few of the covers from the dishes arranged on the tray. There was a steaming dark soup of some kind, and a plate full of herb-crusted pork and vegetables. Some sort of pastry had been arranged on the final plate. I covered my lap with a linen napkin and pulled the soup towards me, imagining it would be glutinous and tasteless. Instead I found it delicious and perfectly spiced. After a few spoons of it, I felt stronger than I had in hours.

"Mmm," I said, and slurped away happily until my bowl was empty, tearing off crusts of bread to mop up the juices. I'd never downed a bowl of soup so fast.

"Sorry," I said, my mouth full. "I'm ravenous."

"So I see," the Colonel said, delicately stroking the side of his mouth. I hastily mopped a spillage with my napkin, loaded the empty bowl onto the tray and started on the main course. This time, I ate a little more slowly.

"You said Queen Victoria sent you out here?" I asked. "What was your mission?"

"Why I should imagine it was much the same as yours." The old man nodded sagely as I cut into the pork.

"I doubt that," I said, coating the chunk of meat on my fork in dark gravy.

"Oh you think Queen Victoria knew nothing of vampires then?"

My fork halted midway to my mouth. I stared at the ghost opposite me in surprise. "You mean she did?"

"Of course. Of course. They'd made some interesting threats against the Royal Family and believe me; the Queen did not suffer fools gladly. We were sent here to make that perfectly plain."

"And did you?" I returned my fork to the plate. "Make it plain, I mean."

"We had the mighty power of the growing Empire behind us. I'd say we stated our case." He hesitated. "Well presumably relations improved, but unfortunately I can't tell you what the final outcome was because I passed away before I could find out."

Fascinating stuff, I thought. I'd love to have known more about Queen Victoria's dealings with Prince Grigor. Definitely something for Mr Kephisto, keeper of stories, to look into when I returned home.

If I returned home.

"I died in this room, you know?" The colonel carried on cheerfully. "I'm becoming a tad bored of it, so it is nice to have company."

"I'll bet," I said, chewing hard on the meat. Too gristly. Monsieur Emietter wouldn't have served up such substandard fayre. It needed roasting more slowly and in a cooler oven. "Have many people stayed in this room."

"A few. Some of them have been interesting. I've had visitors from around the world. Russia, India, Brazil, Mexico, the United States. But I was never able to converse with them until your predecessor showed up."

That stopped me in my tracks once more. "My predecessor?"

"Yes. You must be related somehow. You look a little alike. Just the hair is rather different." He made a gesture around his own head suggesting mine was quite... unkempt. "But given you share the same name I'd say that's a given."

"Alfhild Daemonne?" I checked with him, almost choking on a mouthful of red cabbage.

He nodded.

"Well I'll be—" I couldn't believe it. Gwyn had been here?

"When was this?" I asked.

"Hmmm. Some time ago. A little while after the war. The first one. Nineteen twenties. Mid nineteen twenties." He took a moment. "Yes. I believe it was 1924."

I can't tell you how reassuring it was to have the Colonel to spend time with in that huge hostile castle. He told me what little he knew about Gwyn's brief stay. Apparently the *Vampiri* had made threats against us before. Gwyn had ventured here with a number of high-ranking witches of the day. She'd stayed maybe forty-eight hours or so and departed in a rush. That was all Archibald could tell me.

But I certainly enjoyed his description of my great-grandmother as she was then. Still in her twenties, and feisty as could be. He told me her hair had been darker than mine, more of a tarnished reddy-brown, but her features were similar. And she was well-spoken—I think the insinuation being that I was not—and well-mannered.

Ah, well.

"Can you tell me about her visit here?" I asked the Colonel and he spent a while ruminating over what he could or should say.

"It didn't end well," he started and faltered.

"In what way?" I pressed.

"I don't entirely know. I'm unsure about her diplomatic mission—"

"So it was official?"

Archibald nodded. "Your great-grandmother didn't say very much. She kept things very close to her chest. But I remember that she attended the castle with two colleagues."

"Mmm?" I wanted to know more. I guessed any diplomatic mission relied on a team rather than a single person, but I might have been wrong.

"Unfortunately her colleagues never made it back home."

I gasped. "What happened to them?"

The colonel shook his head. "No-one knows for certain, but er... I did do a little roaming after the event."

"And?"

The Colonel stared into the fire for some time before answering. "I really don't want to alarm you. It was a very long time ago."

I badly wanted to laugh and say, 'Don't worry! I'm made of strong stuff'. However, increasingly I wasn't so sure that I was, so I didn't.

"Does it bring back awful memories?" I asked quietly, and he nodded.

No witch worth the name would let themselves be taken by a vampire. Not one on one at any rate. Which could only mean grandmama's colleagues on the trip had been ganged up on by the nest of vampires inhabiting this wretched castle. No wonder Gwyn loathed them so much.

"How did my Grandmama manage to escape?" I asked.

"I'm not entirely sure, but I'm certain she had inside help," the ghost told me. This made sense.

"Thank goodness," I said, stifling a yawn and

wondering who it had been that had helped Gwyn. Not that it mattered. Whoever it was wouldn't be alive now, one hundred years later.

I regarded the locked door, toying with the wand in my pocket and thinking of escape. I'd eaten and the dinner had helped the nausea, but I recognised I needed sleep too. I understood that if I wanted to keep my strength up, I had to try, although how I'd sleep after Archibald's information I didn't know.

Tomorrow would provide new opportunities to learn about the *Vampiri*. That's what I'd been sent here for. For now, I'd play their game.

Archibald turned his back while I changed for bed, but as I snuggled down beneath the covers, which felt slightly damp to the touch, I asked him whether he would hang about during the night.

"Only..." I hesitated. "If you could alert me to anything out of the ordinary?" I didn't expressly state that I feared I would be murdered in my bed by some voracious pointy-toothed psychopath. I didn't need to say that. I had that sentiment written all over my face.

"Fear not, dear lady," the colonel said with a gallant dip of his head. "It would be my honour."

"Thank you." I lay on my side and watched the flames in the grate. It occurred to me that the fire had not been fed while I'd been in the room, and yet it hadn't died down. There was magick in this castle in spite of the vampires.

I quite liked the thought of that. It comforted me as I finally dropped off to sleep.

I endured a restless night, not least because I was so hot. The fire didn't die back or go out as it should have done, and the windows didn't open. I normally slept in a cold room with the window open so that Mr Hoo could come and go as he pleased.

I missed my feathery little friend.

Archibald dozed in the corner. Ghosts don't need sleep, but it doesn't stop them napping, as Monsieur Emietter often demonstrated. I dragged myself out of bed and made my way to the window to try to take a look at my surroundings through the coloured glass. It was difficult to gauge the time. Leaden clouds zipped across a grey sky. Below me the valley fell away and a blanket of impressively green pine forest stretched as far as the eye could see. Out on the horizon the Carpathian Mountains loomed large, their caps covered in snow.

I longed to get outside and breathe deeply the

fresh and furious air. I could imagine the taste of the pine on my lips. For half a second I considered whipping my wand out and breaking the window locks.

I spun in alarm at a rattle of a key in the door behind me. In a long white nightdress I'd plundered from the wardrobe—It had probably been worn by some Victorian maid many years ago—I stood and waited.

Not Nadia this time.

A dark-cloaked guard, silent and sinister, and the old peasant woman in her drab brown clothes and white apron.

"Good morning," I offered, but she didn't even look up. She tidied up the tray from the previous evening and replaced it with a new one, then left the room.

"Good morning, Madam." The colonel yawned and stretched. "I trust you slept well."

"Not so well," I grumbled. I sat down at the table and inspected breakfast. I wasn't particularly hungry after eating so late the night before, but I was gagging for a cup of tea. Unfortunately, in their wisdom they had only provided some nondescript apple juice and coffee. I picked at some of the eggs provided and pretty much left everything else.

Bidding Archibald to stay where he was, I ran a

quick bath—there was no shower—and jumped in to scrub away two days' worth of grime. I hadn't submerged myself for longer than thirty seconds when something suddenly occurred to me. I jumped out, dried myself off and dressed rapidly, returning to the bedroom where Archibald stared into the fire.

He'd probably been doing that for decades.

"Nadia didn't bring breakfast," I said.

"The *Vampiri* sleep during the day," Archibald confirmed.

I knew that. Of course I did. "So who was the goon in the cloak that brought up breakfast with the old lady?"

"He's a shadow guard. They keep a group of them here. *The Vampiri* have humans around to ensure the smooth running of the castle during the day and to make sure they are not disturbed while they rest."

"Security guards?" I asked.

"The shadow guards look after the security, that's correct, Madam," Archibald confirmed. "They have other humans as servants."

I narrowed my eyes. "Do these shadow guards have weapons?"

Again. "Some."

"Guns?" I asked and when he looked confused I mimed a gun with two fingers. "Bang bang."

"Oh you mean like muskets?" Archibald shook his head. "Not that I've ever seen although I believe there is a locked cabinet downstairs for such things."

I nodded, thinking. The *Vampiri* wouldn't want too many guns on the loose, because a silver bullet would wreak havoc with their quest for immortality.

I hadn't thought to bring any silver bullets with me, and no-one had provided me with any. That was fine. Ostensibly this was a diplomatic mission.

"Let's go for a little walk," I sang with a smile, and Archibald stared at me in confusion.

"The door is locked, Madam. I mean, that won't prevent me, but you—"

"Have a wand." I brandished my curled and well-sanded wand, a piece of Vance the Ent who guarded the marsh in Speckled Wood. It fit naturally in my hand. It connected me with my home. It grounded me.

"And I'm going to have a little look around."

Heart skipping in my chest, I used a little magick spell I'd seen Silvan utilise from time to time to unlock the door. I crept into the corridor and tried a few of the other doors on my landing. They were all locked. There was nothing for it but to retrace my steps from the previous evening. Back out onto the spiral stone staircase and down to the next landing. The wooden door on this floor opened out to one that was remarkably similar to my own. Feeling a little more relaxed I tried all the doors, always expecting them to be locked. I jumped when one finally opened.

The door swung inwards and knocked against the wall beyond with a loud clatter.

I held my breath, my eyes wide. Standing stock still I waited for someone to start shouting and to give the game away at any moment, but nothing happened. Exhaling slowly, I stepped into the room. Much like mine this had a four-poster bed and a roaring fire.

A woman, her face as white as alabaster, her hair as black as a raven's wing, lay in the bed, a smear of blood on her chin. Morbidly curious, I crept towards her. She might have been dead so still did she lie. Her chest did not rise and fall, and there was no hint of movement at all. I inched even closer, so close that I could reach out and touch her if I wished.

From my position I could clearly make out the

threads of tiny veins that lay just below her skin. She might have been aged anywhere from 18 to 108, it was difficult to tell. When the light from the flames shifted and the shadows changed she appeared strangely and uncannily ancient, but when the light was soft and cast her in shadow, she looked breathtakingly beautiful.

Her hair was the colour of burnished gold and quite took my breath away. My hand hovered in the air above her and I had to fight a compulsion to stroke that fine silk-like mane.

"I wouldn't, Madam." Archibald's soft voice reminded me where I was. "Tis usually best not to disturb them. They are so bad-tempered if they don't get enough sleep."

"I know the feeling," I whispered.

"No need to whisper, Madam. They can't hear us, or indeed anything, till twilight."

"But if I touch them, they'll feel it?"

"I wouldn't want to take the chance, Madam," Archibald replied.

I nodded and backtracked from the room, frightened of waking the sleeping terror, and closed the door softly behind myself.

"Is there a vampire behind every locked door?" I asked Archibald in my hushed tone.

"Yes. Several in some cases. They're very...," he pursed his lips and rolled his eyes, "...sociable."

"How many are we talking about?"

"Occupants?" The colonel gave this some thought. "I would say under normal circumstances approximately three dozen."

"So many?" I shuddered.

"Under normal circumstances. At the moment I might suggest you could triple that number?"

I almost shrieked at the thought. "Triple? Over a hundred here? Right now?"

"At least." The colonel remained calm in the face of my absolute horror. "It wouldn't be unheard of for there to be double that."

Could he really be suggesting that there were between one hundred and two hundred vampires currently inhabiting the castle? That seemed a phenomenal amount. I'd heard of nests containing a dozen or more, but what we had here amounted to the largest gathering known in recent times. There had to be something afoot.

And I was here alone with the exception of Ambassador Rubenscarfe. Could the situation get any worse?

"Where are they all?" I looked around as though I'd be able to see them in their hiding places, through the walls, the floors and the ceilings.

"There's a very big basement in this castle. It's damp. It's cold, it's full of the kind of earth they love to sleep in. They revel in it down there."

That sounded grim. "You said under normal circumstances?" I repeated. "What's so different now?"

Archibald smiled at me as though I were a simple creature. "What's so different? I would think that's obvious, Madam. You're here and they've been waiting for you."

I explored as much of the castle as I dared. I didn't venture into the kitchen as that seemed to be where the mortals were hanging out, and I didn't climb down to the basement as the only entry point for that appeared to be through the kitchen.

I hid under a table on the first balcony, and from a distance examined the massive double front doors. A shadow guard had been positioned here. It wouldn't take much to either distract him or use a spell that would knock him out, but for now it wasn't worth the risk. I couldn't be sure how many others would come running. As for the doors themselves. I couldn't tell from my hiding place for sure, but the locks looked fairly straightforward.

I found this of interest. There was evidence of magick in the castle, but not in some of the areas I might have expected it, such as security. I made a mental note of that. It might be useful intelligence I could use later.

The colonel cleared his throat and I looked his way. He pointed at the nearest window and I understood immediately what he was getting at. The light was failing. Twilight was upon us.

Soon the vampires would be awake.

Nodding at Archibald, I backed away from the balcony and quietly climbed the next flight of stairs, retracing my path along the second-floor corridor to the spiral stone staircase back to the correct floor.

As I reached my room and gently pushed open the door, the torches that lined the corridor and the stairwells suddenly began to blaze.

I quietly closed my door, waved my wand over the locks, listening for the tell-tale rumble of the tumblers. Then I ran across the room and threw myself on my bed.

Which is exactly where I was a few minutes later when Nadia came calling.

I changed in the bathroom away from the watchful eyes of Nadia Cozma and Archibald—although for his part the ghost had chosen to disappear when the vampire arrived at my door. Nadia was dressed soberly, in a dark suit and a pristine white blouse, and she had looked me up and down with a measure of disdain.

"Did you bring an evening gown with you?" she asked, and I stared at her dumbfounded.

"I'm here on a diplomatic mission," I said. "I didn't come all this way to go to a ball."

"It's no matter," she said in her clipped accent. She threw open the wardrobe door and took out a long satin dress in the most gorgeous midnight blue.

"I'm not wearing that." I folded my arms in defiance.

"You can't meet the Prince in what you are wearing," Nadia argued. "He won't grant you a viewing."

'A viewing' made it sound as though I was about to line up at the Louvre Museum to take a look at the Mona Lisa.

"You must hurry," Nadia insisted. "The Ambassador is waiting for you."

I glared at her as she handed me the dress. "It

probably won't fit," I grumbled and made for the bathroom.

"Just put it on here," Nadia said.

"Are you kidding?" I nodded my head brusquely at the shadow guard standing in the doorway. "I'll be two minutes."

Before she could argue I'd dashed into the bathroom and closed the door behind me. There was no lock, but I brandished my wand. "*Clauditis.*" That took care of that.

As is the way of these things the dress actually fit me like a glove. I'd never worn a proper ballgown before, so I almost felt like a princess from a fairy tale. The bodice, snug around my chest and stomach, tightened over the hips, then flared out with yards of skirt. I twisted this way and that making the skirts swish.

The only thing letting me down was my hair. Without a shower I hadn't been able to tame it this morning, and it looked slightly—understatement of the year—flyaway.

"*Pulchra imperdiet,*" I tried and lo! My hair twisted over and up into a beautiful plaited crown. I only needed a tiara and I would have passed for nobility.

"Wow." I marvelled at my appearance, until I heard Nadia at the door.

"Is everything alright? We must attend the Prince. We cannot keep him waiting."

I tried to thrust my wand into my pocket, its habitual hiding place, quickly realising I had a problem. The dress didn't have any; they would have ruined the line. Where could I store it?

With Nadia banging on the door I had to think quickly. I plunged the wand into my cleavage and pushed it down out of sight. I'd have to be careful not to bend over too far or it would snap.

Nadia nodded appreciatively when I let myself out of the bathroom. "Splendid," she muttered, "and now we must hurry."

I followed her as she rushed down the spiral staircase, amazed that she could move so quickly on those impossible heels she was wearing. *Click, click, click* went her shoes as I struggled to keep up in my much flatter leather lace-up boots.

We raced along the corridor on the second floor and then down the slightly-less-grand staircase. Once we were on the first floor we slowed down. Nadia rolled her shoulders, lifted her chin and stretched her back, walking with a succinctly sexy swagger. Obviously she intended to impress Prince Grigor. Perhaps she wanted a new role as one of his wives, or maybe she had simply perfected the art of walking with grace and elegance.

Gruesome.

I clumped along a little distance behind her. Once I'd navigated the final staircase beneath the billowing chandelier, I was somewhat pleased to see Ambassador Rubenscarfe waiting for us, a hooded *Vampiri* shadow guard in tow.

"Ah, Alfhild. Thank goodness." The Ambassador sounded a little shaky of voice. "I trust you have been treated well?"

"Very well." I tried to reassure him. "Fed and watered and..." I glanced at Nadia, "... I've had plenty of sleep."

"That's good. It's an unusual... ah... precedent they've set... locking us in our rooms."

I shrugged, pretending I hadn't really noticed. "Like I said, I've been asleep most of the day."

The Ambassador nodded; his face troubled. He turned to address Nadia once more. "I brought gifts. Sent by Mother Neamh. They came in the limousine with us."

"Do not worry, Ambassador." Nadia nodded at one of the hooded shadow guards who himself turned and clicked his fingers, thereby summoning several people who scampered towards us carrying an assortment of chests and treasures. "I have your gifts."

Nadia looked at me. "Shall we go in? Prince Grigor is keen to make your acquaintance."

CHAPTER TEN

It soon became clear why I'd been compelled to throw on a posh frock. We were shown through a side door into a magnificent medieval banqueting hall with the largest fireplace I had ever seen. In fact, I had fireplace envy. You could have drawn a horse and carriage underneath the mantlepiece of the beast in this room and still had space for The Devonshire Fellows to sit on top and play a set of madrigals. Huge chunks of tree trunk burned in the grate and acted as an additional source of illumination for the room.

The room was colossal. No wonder you almost burst a lung climbing the mountainous grand staircase in the entrance hall outside. A pair of crystal chandeliers hung high above my head and the ceiling had been vaulted, like something you might see in a church or cathedral. Painted panels depicted colourful characters having a great time in ways most normal people might not necessarily have approved of. I stared in fascination for a second at a scene depicting Death throwing its skeletal arms around a bunch of naked humans, and then hastily looked away in search of something a little more wholesome.

As in my bedroom, huge tapestries hung from the walls. Once these would have been bright with colour, but time had dulled the threads and the culminated effects of soot from the fire and tallow from the candles had contrived to mask their beauty. It seemed a shame not to have them cleaned and cared for, but I had a feeling that if I studied the drapes too closely I might not approve of their subject matter either.

At the top end of the room stood a raised dais, where a table had been set. There were several other long tables arranged in front of this stage area, and here people were milling about in all their glorious finery. I spied an interesting array of silk, satin, feathers, and leather and lace on display, with varying sizes of ruffs competing with plunging necklines, absurd wigs and oversize fans made from ostrich feathers. These people clearly felt most comfortable in clothes from their own eras.

My heart fluttered nervously in my chest. So this

was what a nest of vampires looked like close up. Some of these monsters were hundreds of years old, and yet all of them, with their pale waxy skin and dead eyes, had a beauty rarely seen on the flushed faces of our own youthful supermodels. I could only imagine that if you were immortal and you desired a new playmate or partner, you picked your companions from the most stunning the human race had to offer at any one time.

Besides, most vampires seemed to have accumulated an obscene amount of wealth. They happily moved in the higher echelons of society, in social circles I could only dream about as they sucked the life from many a human.

I wondered if this was how Queen Victoria had come to know of their existence and if that was why Archibald Peters had been sent here to Castle Iadului on his mission.

Nadia cleared her throat next to me. "If you would be so kind to step this way, Miss Daemonne? Ambassador Rubenscarfe?"

She led us closer to the dais, and we followed in her wake. I could sense that the Ambassador's reluctance was almost as great as my own, because he dawdled a little. A hooded shadow guard prodded him in the back to get him moving again.

I hadn't previously noticed but, sitting on a chair —slumped really—was a small old man. A wizened almost skeletal man with skin as tanned as ancient leather. Below wispy white eyebrows, his sunken black eyes glared out at me with a loathing he didn't bother to disguise.

"Prince Grigor," Nadia bowed deeply. "If it pleases you, here is the diplomatic party from the British Ministry of Witches."

She turned her head sideways and nodded at me expectantly. I returned her look blankly. Was I supposed to say something? *Do* something? What precisely? This Prince Grigor didn't exactly look like he would be receptive to my greetings.

Fortunately the Ambassador had been trained for this situation. He took the lead. Stepping forwards he took my elbow and led me even closer to the dais. He bowed deeply, and I followed his lead.

"Good evening to you, Prince Grigor. I am Ambassador Rubenscarfe. This is my young protégé, Alfhild Daemonne."

The old man's eyes glittered when he heard my name and he pushed himself weakly upright to get a better look at me.

"Well, well, well," he rasped and there was something in his voice that made my toes curl with revulsion. It sounded like something reptilian slithering over ancient parchment, or the dry rustle of the mummified skin of a long dead ancient Pharaoh.

I fixed a pleasant look to my face, although it hurt me to do so.

"The owner of Whittle Inn?" The prince directed this question at Nadia and she nodded.

"Yes, my Prince."

He smiled, evidently as difficult for him as it was for me, although in his case it looked as though rigor mortis had set in. He appraised me with those demonic eyes of his and my insides recoiled in disgust while all the time I stood still and tried to maintain a pleasant and calm expression.

Would now be a good time to raise the issue of Thaddeus? Maybe lament his loss and explain it had nothing to do with me?

Apparently not.

The Ambassador jumped in before I could do or say anything.

"Your Grace, if I may." He glanced behind at the servants who had followed us into the hall bearing the goods we had brought with us. "Mother Neamh, the Mother of all Witches sent you a wonderful array of gifts she thought you might appreciate."

He took the first one, an intricately carved

leather box with magick symbols embossed on the front, and placed it on the dais in front of Prince Grigor. "Here we have a portable medicinal potionery." He struggled to open it, so I stepped forward and helped him. It opened out to reveal four sections, each with three shelves laden with tiny potion bottles. I glanced at the potions with interest. Millicent would have a greater understanding of them all than I, but I did recognise *Fevergrippe* and *Pain-ease*, as two standard potions any witch worth her salt kept in her bathroom. As for the others, there was nothing there you wouldn't give a child to play with. These would be safe with vampires and not add to their powers.

Prince Grigor looked under-impressed, as well he might. The portable medicinal potionery was an expensive first aid kit and nothing more. Behind us, the hall remained still, an icy chill in the air.

Evidently we needed to do more to impress this man.

The second gift comprised a small chest chock-full of crystals. Some of these were ten-a-penny in many high street shops, but I recognised a few others that were much rarer. Many witches derived power from their crystal work, and a few choice crystals used properly can greatly enhance the potency of a spell or a ritual. This seemed a generous gift.

The colours, picked up by the candles, dazzled as the box was turned around to show the Prince. He appeared a little more appreciative of this.

The third gift seemed to be an oddity at first glance. A child's toy theatre, standing around three feet in height, complete with a proscenium arch front. Ambassador Rubenscarfe demonstrated how to raise the safety curtain and behind it were several puppets, dressed in Elizabethan garb, perhaps performing some Shakespearian comedy.

Ambassador Rubenscarfe located a little switch to the side of the wooden structure and suddenly the puppets came alive, moving around the stage, each in its own spotlight, gesturing grandly at each other and the audience.

"Quite entrancing." Prince Grigor obviously approved of this. He looked about at his nest of vampires and they laughed and exclaimed on cue. The atmosphere in the hall visibly lightened and I drew in a shaky breath. I hadn't realised how tense I'd been feeling, but now I allowed myself some hope that I'd get out of this little Transylvanian escapade unscathed.

Prince Grigor nodded at Nadia who turned and

clapped her hands. Musicians in a gallery above our heads began to play. The chamber orchestra produced a dirge-like baroque composition. Not a patch of the Devonshire Fellows and their joyous squashed-goose music, I decided, feeling suddenly and desperately homesick and much more appreciative of Luppitt's compositions.

"Prince Grigor would like you to join him at the table for tonight's banquet," Nadia told me, gesturing for me to climb onto the dais and take my seat next to him. The Ambassador was shown to a seat on the other side.

I perched on the hard wood chair and attempted another smile when the prince turned my way. I couldn't get past his appearance. His thick lips glinted in the light because he dribbled constantly like a geriatric not quite in charge of all his bodily functions. A subtle tang of slightly tainted meat filled the air around him. It had been a long time since breakfast, but even so I wasn't entirely sure I'd be able to eat.

To the right of me, a young vampire, introduced to me as Count Ivan Yorovski, tried to engage me in conversation. His hair was a shock of blonde, his eyes as blue as the summer sky over Whittlecombe. He was probably handsome, but I was too distracted by the length of his canines when he smiled to notice. I shrank into myself, trying not to share too much about my life in England.

I kept half an ear on the Ambassador's conversation while watching several vampires dance on the floor below us, entertaining their own kind in front of dining tables which groaned with the weight of food that probably none of them would eat. Some of the more glamorous beings danced along to the orchestra with the sincerity expected of the period—graceful and elegant—while others, evidently turned into vampires much more recently, hammed it up. Men danced with women, women with women, men with men. It seemed that here at Castle Iadului anything went. I didn't object to this at all. But I couldn't help fearing that the night could lead to a descent into hedonism I wanted no part of, and from which it might be difficult to extract myself in one piece.

The soup, as with the previous evening, was perfectly edible. I wasn't sure what flavour it was, but it warmed my insides and eased my hunger pangs. If I didn't lean into the prince or inhale, I could eat without too much nausea.

Wine was poured into our goblets, Count Yorovski waved the decanter at me every few minutes and I politely declined, merely sipping at mine. I wanted to keep all my faculties about me. The Ambassador laughed at a joke someone—perhaps even Prince Grigor—had made. I turned my attention back to them, understanding the necessity of appearing eager and interested.

Isn't that what diplomacy is all about, after all?

"This is a splendid feast you have treated us to. We cannot thank you enough. You really must consider visiting us in London, your Grace," the ambassador was saying in his most conniving and sycophantic tone. "Mother Neamh would be delighted to receive you and I can assure you of the warmest and most magickal of welcomes."

The prince moved his lips into what might have been a smile.

"We would treat you to a full range of delights, as well as showing you the all the sights that London has to offer," the Ambassador chirruped on. Even I found him annoying and we were both on the same side. "Have you ever been to London, your Grace?"

"Several times. Long ago," Prince Grigor rasped. "And elsewhere in the British Isles since then."

I looked sideways at him, pondering.

He caught me looking and leered, shifting in his seat so that he could breathe into my face. "Such an enquiring mind you have, Miss Daemonne. Are you curious as to where I have visited?"

"I was wondering when you were in London," I replied, forcing a bright smile. "The capital has changed so much over the years."

"This I have heard although I have not seen for myself. The last time I was there, Queen Victoria sat on her throne. I courted one of her daughters."

I couldn't hide my shock. He'd had the audacity to date one of the royal princesses? No wonder Colonel Peters had been dispatched to Transylvania. Imagine the scandal if a royal princess had been turned into a vampire.

Prince Grigor threw his head back and laughed, phlegm or something equally hideous, gurgling in his throat. "Bless you, child." Prince Grigor reached out with a dry bony hand to pat my arm. "If you only knew the half of it."

As badly as I wanted to extricate my arm from beneath his vile touch I held myself very still and nodded as if bowled over by his words. Fortuitously, we were interrupted by the arrival of the main course. A boar's head.

Each.

Served on a wooden platter. With an apple in its mouth and a side of red cabbage.

I prodded the head with my fork. Count Yurovski handed me a sharp knife with a wooden handle. "You'll need this," he said. "Remove the skull and you'll find the brain underneath."

I groaned quietly, but smiled my thanks at him, momentarily considering plunging the knife in his eye, but in a room full of vampires, the last thing you want to do is strike the first blow. Especially when you're supposed to be making nice with them.

"I'm not really that hungry," I lied, and forked a spoonful of red cabbage into my mouth instead.

That, at least, was delicious.

"I think that went rather well, don't you?" Ambassador Rubenscarfe paused at the top of the grand staircase before being led to his own chamber.

"I certainly hope so," I replied. I couldn't tell whether it had, or it hadn't. While I'd been sitting at the long table on the dais taking in the dancers below, my witchy senses had noted the undercurrents of emotions; quietly uttered conversations, secretive looks and muttered oaths. All things that had eluded me yet evidently veiled certain sinister intentions. "We are still effectively prisoners here after all." I gestured at the eavesdropping Nadia who stood close by, and the hooded security guards, their faces hidden from view. "I think we should still be watchful."

The Ambassador nodded. "Nevertheless, I'm sure I can report to Mother Neamh that tensions have eased a little now that Prince Grigor has had the chance to make your acquaintance."

"Do you think we'll be able to leave tomorrow?" I couldn't help the note of yearning. Castle Iadului completely unnerved me and I wanted to go home. To my inn. To Speckled Wood. To my friends and Mr Hoo.

"We'll have one more audience with the prince tomorrow evening and then yes, I should think we can wrap things up to everyone's satisfaction." Ambassador Rubenscarfe nodded, obviously pleased with himself.

I bid him goodnight and allowed myself to be led to the left, the long corridor and the winding stone staircase by my silent guard. I climbed the steps wearily, imagining how the party was unravelling in the Great Hall downstairs. Archibald had been right after all. Tonight I'd be grateful for all the locks on my door.

My hooded guard pushed open the door, stepped

back and let me through. Once I was inside he backed away, closed the door and locked it. I stepped further inside. The room was exactly as I'd left it.

Almost.

There was a tray on the table. Not the breakfast tray but a lunch tray.

The old peasant woman had been in my room to take away the breakfast tray and replace it with a lunch tray.

While I'd been out of the room earlier today.

I hadn't had time to notice when I'd come back from my foray around the castle, and because Archibald had been with me, he hadn't alerted me to the visit either.

Presumably she hadn't been back with a supper tray because she knew I'd be at the banquet this evening.

My stomach lurched. Unless she had assumed I was in the bathroom she had to know I hadn't been in the room when I should have been. And because one of the shadow guards always accompanied her, he knew that too.

Surely they'd have reported it?

"Is everything alright, Madam?" Colonel Peters apparated next to me. "You seem a little shaken."

"It hasn't been the most pleasant of evenings," I

told him, eyeing the tray with trepidation. "The Prince—" I grimaced.

"Ah yes, Madam. Not a pleasant creature."

I shook my head. "Why do all the rest of the vampires look so gorgeous and glamorous and he looks like..." I struggled to come up with a parallel.

"Something a cat chewed up?" suggested the Colonel.

"Worse." I pulled a face.

"I believe it's because somewhere along the line he may have consumed bad blood of some sort and that has affected his cell regeneration."

That seemed a plausible theory. "But the others? It doesn't affect them?"

The colonel shrugged. "The Prince gets the prime choice of morsels when he hunts. The others are left with the dregs. He has the best of everything. Many of his companions and wives have decayed beyond usefulness and have gone to dust. Either by their own volition," he scratched the end of his nose delicately, "or his."

I winced. *The murdering toad.* The sooner I found a way out of this castle the better.

"I think the prince is nearing the end of his time, Madam."

Not absolutely immortal then?

"Colonel?" I made my way over to the table and looked down at the silver platter covered dishes. "What do you know about the woman who brings the meals up from the kitchen?"

"Not a huge amount," the colonel admitted. "She lives in the village down the road. You probably passed it on your way here.

I thought back to the lonely winding road through the forest. There hadn't been much to see. I vaguely recalled a few lonely buildings.

"She's not a vampire. Is she sympathetic to them?"

The colonel shook his head. That made sense. She didn't fit the mode. Didn't look like one of them and had none of their swagger and arrogance. "Remember, they hire locals to help out with the daily running of the castle. In many cases they have little choice."

"I see." Yes, he'd told me that.

Perhaps she hadn't said anything to the vampires about my absence after all. Maybe she wasn't even on their side.

I lifted one of the silver domes off its plate, idly wondering what had been for lunch and whether any cake had been on the menu.

The plate was empty of everything except a folded piece of paper.

I gaped at in in surprise, then dropped the dome with a clang in my rush to pick up the note and read what it had to say.

Meet me on the roof at midnight.

It had been signed by 'A friend.'

CHAPTER ELEVEN

I huddled in a sheltered place where two of the outer walls met. With little time to change I'd simply thrown a robe over my satin dress, checked my wand was safely in place, grabbed my mobile and crept out of my room. While off on my wanderings earlier in the day, I hadn't ventured up to the roof, but I figured it wouldn't be difficult to find. One simply carried on climbing the stairs, I supposed. In effect that was all I needed to do; round and round for what seemed an interminable amount of time. The stairwells became increasingly narrow and the steps themselves more uneven as though no great care had been taken over the crafting of these.

Eventually I could go no further. I paused and held my ear against the wood of the final door for a long time, trying to ascertain what was on the other side. There was nothing but silence, and the cold draft coming from the crack at the foot of the door suggested I'd reached my final destination.

I gently eased the door open and slipped out into the brisk night. Finding nobody about, I scoured the shadows. The moon was out somewhere. I could tell because the mountains in the distance seemed to be lit with a most unearthly glow. But above me the clouds were thick, and very little light penetrated the shadows.

There were several towers dotted about among the low battlements. As far as I could see they weren't inhabited, or if they were, the sentries must have been asleep.

I took out my mobile and switched it on, waiting for it to warm up, remembering belatedly the annoying little tune it made as it switched itself on. I jammed it into my stomach, dropped into a crouch and tried to cover the noise, using my body as sound proofing. It still sounded ridiculously loud under the cover of quiet darkness.

Still nobody came.

I waited until I was certain all was clear before thumbing the screen. I quickly muted the sound and studied the display. Would I get a signal up here?

One bar.

Then it dropped out again.

I tutted, lifted the phone and waved it around.

One bar!

And out it went again.

"Batpoop," I cursed.

I left my sheltered corner and meandered into the centre of the roof, twisting the phone this way and that. If my orb wouldn't work this would be my only means of reaching someone at home. In an ideal world that would mean Wizard Shadowmender, but I guessed that I'd probably have to make do with Penelope Quigwell.

One bar!

Nothing ventured, nothing gained. I found Penelope's number and tried to dial. No joy. The signal dropped out and the call failed.

"Uh." I groaned, lifting my arm once more to catch the illusive signal I so desperately needed. I pivoted to my right and ran smack bang into a solid man chest.

My mobile flew from my grasp. Reeling backwards I opened my mouth to scream. A huge gloved hand reached out and clamped its palm over my mouth.

Eyes wide I stared up into the masked face of

one of the hooded shadow guards. His eyes glinted as they bore into mine.

Not a vampire, I thought. *Too alive for that but I'm done for all the same. He'll turn me in and Alfhild will be Prince Grigor's late night supper.*

I twisted viciously, trying to loosen the man's grip on me. Simultaneously I stamped my foot down hard on his. He swore at me and his grasp eased. It gave me the minutest of advantages. I tried to reach for my wand, still hidden down my bodice. A sharp familiar voice growled at me.

"I wouldn't if I were you, Alfhild. You know I'm a darn sight faster on the draw than you are."

I scuttled backwards in shock. "Silvan?" I cried, and clamped my own hands over my mouth, fearful that someone would hear us. He reached out and pulled me close. How had I not realised? His height, the breadth of him, even his scent. So recognisable. So very Silvan.

The strength disappeared from my knees, more from relief than any continuing terror.

"I thought you were one of them," I babbled. He reached out and stroked my cheek with his gloved hand. "I thought you'd abandoned me. Gone off gallivanting."

"I would never do that," he soothed.

"I've been feeling so alone here. Terrified," I admitted to him. When he pulled me into his chest and held me, I let him for once, all the fight gone out of me. "We were supposed to be accompanied by security guards but Ambassador Rubenscarfe let them go."

"Did he? That's strange." He pondered on this. "If I were you I'd be careful around him. You've been taking too many risks. Why can't you just stay in your room?"

"I want to get away. I didn't come here by choice. I don't know why they've sent me." I pulled back a little so I could look at him, although it was disconcerting staring at a man in a mask. He didn't look much like Silvan at all.

"The Ministry of Witches are trying to draw out the real murderer," Silvan told me.

"You mean of Thaddeus?" I pulled away and glared at him in suspicion. "How do you know that?"

"Because Wizard Shadowmender told me."

That news hit me like a bolt from the blue. "Wizard Shadowmender told you that? He didn't tell me. Why did he tell you? Since when did you become so friendly with him?"

"He hired me," Silvan replied, his voice calm and quiet.

"He hired you?" I thought about this, shaking my head at his totally incredulous story.

Silvan reached for my hand. "He offered to pay me good money to come over here in advance of you and get myself hired. I had a couple of days to sort it all out. They're always looking for decent guards at this castle given how remote it is and the rather demanding nature of the client."

"I see." That's why he was here. Wizard Shadowmender had sent him. And Silvan had wanted the money.

It was stupid to feel so hurt, given the dangerous situation I found myself in, but I did, nevertheless.

"I see," I repeated again and blinked back tears. How ridiculous. I pulled myself together and stepped away, casting about for my mobile. "So is there a plan?" I asked not looking at him.

"Not really," Silvan replied, and his voice sounded strangely thick. "I just wanted you to know I was here, and to tell you not to take any more risks."

"Well gee thanks," I retorted. "That helps loads."

"I thought it might," Silvan returned, his voice gently mocking me.

For some reason that made me feel a little better. It offered an edge of normality to the chaotic new world I found myself in.

"Help me find my phone," I demanded. "I dropped it when you grabbed me. It must be here somewhere."

I failed to find the phone. I could only hope that it remained hidden from any sentries who patrolled the roof during the day and that it didn't suddenly find a signal and start picking up messages and texts. Thank goodness I'd switched the sound off.

Silvan and I had parted ways, with me gruffly wishing him a good night and him laughing quietly. I'd returned to my room where Colonel Peters was waiting for me, agog to hear we had a friend on the inside.

As I lay in bed, watching the flames dance in the grate, I couldn't help thinking he wasn't the only one. I hadn't asked Silvan about the elderly peasant lady, but it stood to reason that she had covered for me too. I felt better knowing I had a few friends around me. After all, I didn't know whether the Ambassador had the capacity to pull off this diplomatic mission or not.

The more I considered it, the more I recognised the existence of magick in the castle. The fires that burned without needing to be tended, the torches in the stone hallways that burst into flame of their own volition. If this had been a game of *Double Jeopardy* and someone had described those two acts, I would have known the answer right away.

Something a witch can do.

Chapter Twelve

"What are you doing in here?" Ambassador Rubenscarfe knotted the cord of his heavy robe in consternation. It complemented the colours in the tapestries hanging in this bed chamber. He'd obviously only climbed out of the bath recently. His face was pink from the steam, and his hair and beard were damp. He looked scrubbed clean like a baby, almost vulnerable.

"I thought we should have a little tete-a-tete," I said, eyeing his breakfast tray. I'd eaten all of mine, but I could still have gone another round of toast and more coffee. Unfortunately, although the Ambassador had left plenty of food, it all looked a little cold and sad.

"I thought we were locked in?" he hissed at me.

"Well we are. Or were," I replied, and gestured at my own witchy robes with a dramatic sweep of my wand. "For are we not witches? Can we not undo locks with a spell?" How had he failed to notice that?

"It's just not respectful," the Ambassador blustered, and I frowned at him. Surely he didn't intend to simply roll over and allow Grigor and his band of evil followers to do what they wanted with us and limit our freedoms?

"How is locking us in our rooms respectful?" I asked. "I put up with it for one night for the sake of our 'mission', but I've no intention of being cowed by these people."

He had no answer to that. I threw myself down on his sofa in front of yet another gaily burning fire. Not a basket of logs in sight in this room either. "What's the plan?" I demanded.

"Plan?" he repeated, and I rolled my eyes.

"Why does nobody have a plan?" I asked him.

Ambassador Rubenscarfe came to join me, perching on the sofa. "Probably because we don't need one."

"Of course we need one." I jabbed my finger in his direction. "You're assuming that Prince Grigor has accepted our gifts as peace offerings and that tonight he'll give his blessing to an ongoing Vampire Nation and Ministry of Witches peace pact." I sat back and folded my arms. "I really can't see that happening."

"There have been no indicators to the contra—"

"There's been every indication! We're prisoners here! We need an escape plan for when it all goes wrong."

"If everything goes wrong I'm sure Wizard Shadowmender will come up with a way to rescue us." Ambassador Rubenscarfe pursed his lips—it really didn't suit him.

"You mean as happened in 1924?" I asked.

The Ambassador's ruddy face seemed to grow suddenly pale. "How do you know about that?"

"I have a source."

"Clearly." The ambassador turned sharp eyes on me. "Someone who is speaking out of turn. Who would that be?"

I ignored his query. "Why out of turn?"

"What happened back then—the death of those two witches—was a mistake."

I sucked in my breath. This sounded worse than I'd imagined. "The death of two witches?"

"I thought you said you knew all about it." The ambassador glared at me.

"Well I know a bit, but—"

The ambassador waved his hands to quieten me. "It's all hush, hush. A terrible error."

"Especially for the poor witches." I grimaced. These were Gwyn's colleagues? If so it appeared she'd escaped from certain death. "The prince can obviously not be trusted."

"The *Vampiri* have sworn that it will never happen again. We are quite safe. I can assure you of that."

I puffed out my cheeks in exasperation. The ambassador's assurances weren't worth a jot, evidently. How could he trust these monstrous creatures? To me, they appeared to be completely without honour.

He narrowed his eyes at me. "You said 'why does *nobody* have a plan'. Who besides us do you think is without a plan?"

"Well the shadow guard of course," I answered. He had to know about Silvan. He was leading the mission and I assumed Wizard Shadowmender wouldn't keep him in the dark.

"Which shadow guard?" he asked with genuine bemusement and I realised I'd made a mistake.

I backtracked quickly. If Wizard Shadowmender hadn't informed Ambassador Rubenscarfe about Silvan then presumably there was a good reason for that. "I thought Wizard Shadowmender was sending some security personnel out here with us?" I feigned alarm.

The Ambassador gave me a hard look while I tried not to wriggle like a fish caught on a hook.

"No? I guess we're on our own then?" I said, and he grunted.

He cleared his throat and glanced at the door. "There's absolutely nothing for you to worry about, Alfhild."

All of a sudden the heat of the fire stifled me, and I broke out in a sweat. Something was amiss here. I stood and hastily took my leave, more certain than ever that, in spite of Ambassador Rubenscarfe's protestations to the contrary, I had plenty to worry about.

When Nadia turned up at my door later that evening and queried my choice of clothing once more, I sighed. Tonight's gown, selected by her from the wardrobe—in glorious forest green—definitely showed me for what I was. I couldn't imagine a vampire wearing such an obviously witchy colour.

I changed in the bathroom again, marvelling at

the fact that Nadia had a selection of clothes to choose from that were exactly my size. Personally I'd have happily worn my robes to any occasion at any time, but apparently that was frowned upon in most civilised corners and I was required to dress myself up like a dog's dinner. I couldn't help but think this was more for the malodourous delectation of the prince and his ghastly hangers' on than for proprieties' sake.

Not that I considered these vampires civilised in any way, shape or form of course.

Just one more dinner, I told myself, *that's all!* Then with any luck I would be on a plane and heading back to Whittlecombe in the morning.

Feeling slightly less nervous than I had the previous night I trailed after Nadia and the hooded shadow guard. I checked the man's gait and size, and while he was tall, he was definitely stouter than Silvan. En route, we met up with the Ambassador. He seemed even twitchier than he had been the night before and struggled to make eye contact with me. He slipped ahead of me, so I followed in his wake, frowning at the back of his head, wondering about his apparent rudeness. A long line of shadow guards fell in behind us, escorting us as we made our way down the stairs.

"Is everything alright, Ambassador Rubenscarfe?" I asked him when we paused outside the door of The Great Hall and he could no longer ignore my existence.

"It's fine, Miss Daemonne. Absolutely fine." He smiled a non-smile, still without looking at me.

"If you're worried about earlier—" I began, but the doors opened, and we were ushered through, the shadow guards marching in our wake and arranging themselves in two lines behind us. I observed this with a frown. What was going on here? Nadia's face wore a harried expression which I put down to us being slightly late. I hadn't gone more than half a dozen steps when I realised that the atmosphere inside The Great Hall differed greatly to what we'd 'enjoyed' the previous evening.

The fire burned dully and gave off no warmth. The tables had been dismantled and removed, so that the wooden floor was a simple plain expanse. Tonight the chandeliers had not been lit, and so the supplementary light for that vast cathedral-like room, came from a few dozen tall candles. Prince Grigor sat alone on his throne on the dais, slumped almost into insignificance, but his eyes glittered hungrily as we advanced towards him.

I'd thought the hall devoid of his followers, but in

the shadows, where the fire and the inadequate candlelight could not reach, I heard the rustle of silk, and by reaching out with my senses I could hear and feel the ultra-slow heart beats of several dozen of Grigor's wretched followers.

The Ambassador and I were urged on, and we walked slowly between two lines of the hooded and masked guards. I badly wanted to find Silvan, to seek his reassurance, but the guard following me struck me on the shoulder when I dallied. I stumbled and almost fell.

Alarmed, I tried to turn about, ready to give him a piece of my mind. What did he think he was doing? But before I could speak, he kicked out at the back of my legs, and I fell into a kneeling position, prostate before the Prince of the Corinthians.

I cried out in surprise and pain and tried once more to turn my head to search for Silvan, but the shadow guard clipped me around the ear. My hair, that I'd spent all of twenty seconds trying to perfect with my hair-tidy spell, came loose from its moorings and spilled out around my shoulders.

"Ah! Such beauty, Alfhild Daemonne." Grigor oozed forwards in his chair and gazed down at me. "I can't help feeling you'd make a spectacular vampire." He reached out with a gnarled leathery hand, his horribly long nails were yellow with age and hooked into claws. He crooked one finger at me, beckoning me closer with his obscene digit. "Wouldn't you care to join us, Alfhild? Join my merry nest. You'd be the brightest of all my wives."

Needless to say, my response wasn't polite. "No. I would not."

"Such a shame. Such a wasted opportunity." His slobber-coated tongue performed a complete circuit of his revolting lips, then he raised his limp wrist and beckoned. "Ambassador?"

Ambassador Rubenscarfe came forward, bowing so deeply he might have been dusting the wooden floorboards with his nose. "Your Grace?"

"Please explain to Miss Daemonne what will happen next."

"Me, your Grace?" he asked.

Prince Grigor smiled, genuinely enjoying what was unfolding in front of him. "Indeed Ambassador. Be the bearing of our glad tidings."

The Ambassador turned to me and I spotted fear in his eyes. "Ah, Alfhild. I... er... His Grace would like you to stand trial for the death of Thaddeus Corinthian."

My insides turned to water. This was exactly

what I had feared. I swallowed hard. "Ambassador—"

"I apologise. It is completely out of my hands."

"What?" I tried to stand, only to be pushed down by the over-zealous shadow guard standing behind me. "You can't allow them to do this. Wizard Shadowmender will—"

"Wizard Shadowmender is unreachable." The Ambassador shrugged, helplessly. "The goddess knows I have tried to reach him, but to no avail." He regarded me with a certain amount of cunning. "I'm sure you have tried too."

I had on numerous occasions. The orb remained silent. My mobile phone lost on the roof somewhere. They were purposely blocking all my attempts at communication.

"But you know—you *must* know—that there is no way he would allow this!" I stared at the ambassador, confused by his bearing. He'd obviously known Grigor was planning this. Why when had they spoken together, had the ambassador not expressly forbidden it? It would cause the worst kind of diplomatic incident. The Ministry of Witches would be up in arms.

The Ambassador turned away from me. "You forget yourself, Miss Daemonne. Wizard Shadowmender holds no authority in these parts, or even over the diplomatic service. It is I who am in charge of our mission here, and in the interests of peace between The Vampire Nation and ourselves, I say you must stand trial, just as Prince Grigor wishes."

"You cannot give into him!" With fury I launched myself at the Ambassador's legs.

"Guards, guards!" he shrieked in a high-pitch wail, as though he thought I could do any real damage to him. They were on me in seconds. In spite of struggling with them, they had my hands behind me and tied painfully tight in no time. They dragged me back to the centre of the floor in front of the dais and forced me to kneel once more before the prince. He eyed me as though I were a tasty delicacy he would savour for his supper.

"Her wand?" he enquired, and Nadia spoke from behind me.

"There are no pockets in the gown, my Prince. I made quite sure of that. She must have left it in her bedroom."

"Very good. See that it is located and destroyed." The prince spoke into the shadows. "Ilya?"

I heard the tell-tale tip-tapping of a woman's shoes as someone moved across the floor behind me.

She came to stand directly next to me and bowed. "My Prince?"

Grigor nodded at her. "You will act as my counsel."

"It will be the highest honour of my life, my Prince," she murmured politely. Perfect English without the trace of an accent. I turned my head a little to get a better look. Slender with a glorious wave of black silken hair. If I wasn't much mistaken this was the beautiful vampire I'd found sleeping during my first foray around the castle.

She turned to me and confirmed my thought. Skin as pale as any statue, the veins faint below the surface. Lips of blood red. Her black eyes met my green ones and as she drew her lips back in a smile I caught a glimpse of pointed canines.

"Wait," I said.

"You will be given an opportunity to state your case," Ilya informed me, not unkindly.

"But where is the judge? Where are the jury? How will I have a fair trial?" I demanded, shuffling forward on my knees in fury.

Grigor struggled into a standing position and flung his arms open. "Well I'm the judge, of course. Who else?" He clapped his hands and the rustling in the shadows increased. I heard titters and cat calls. I dared to cast another glance that way, my ear still hot from the last slap I'd received. Vampires shifted on the dark edges of the light. I couldn't make out whole forms, just the glint of teeth and several pairs of cold burning eyes.

"They can be the jury if you insist on having one, Alfhild." He played with my name, caressing the syllables, drooling over the plosive D.

I shivered in revulsion.

"Enough procrastination," he announced. He gestured at Ilya. "Begin!"

"I put it to you that during the early hours of the morning of 29th of October last year, Miss Daemonne, you held Thaddeus Corinthian against his will and then, knowing full well what would happen, when the sun rose you exposed him to its rays and watched him die. The charge against you is wilful destruction of a vampire." Ilya had a clipboard and she referred to it as she spoke.

I cast my mind back to that awful morning when I'd come downstairs to find the lights had fused. What had happened next was etched on my retina forever. Horrendous. I'd been traumatised by the vision of Thaddeus burning up and shrivelling to dust ever since.

I swallowed.

"How do you plead, Miss Daemonne?" Ilya asked.

"Not guilty." I heard the tremor in my voice.

"We can't hear you." Prince Grigor already sounded bored. If he became too fed up I was liable to be found guilty in record time.

"Not guilty," I repeated, louder this time and with an attempt at a swagger that I didn't feel.

"Well, let me take you back. Thaddeus Corinthian was a guest at your inn, was he not?"

I nodded. There were certain facts I would not be able to dispute. "He was."

"And when did you first meet him?"

I thought back. "I can't be exactly sure, but it would have been around the 25th or 26th October. The whole wedding party—"

"This was the wedding of Melchior Laurent and Ekaterina Lukova?"

"Yes. I'd agreed to host Melchior's wedding. It had been scheduled for Samhain."

Ilya wrote something on her notes. "So you met Thaddeus on 25th of October?"

"Not exactly," I said, remembering the line of

hearses turning up on my drive, the blue of the gas lamps and the sound of the gravel scattering around the drive outside the front of my beloved wonky inn. "The instructions I was given, by a driver, ordered me to store the coffins in the cellar, even though I had rooms ready. I didn't see any of them till after the sun had set the following night."

"So you first met Thaddeus on 26th of October?"

"That's correct." *Glad we've sorted that out*, I thought.

"And what did you think of him?"

"What?" I couldn't imagine being asked such a question in a British court. That wouldn't have been an objective question and it would only have produced a subjective reaction. "You can't ask me that."

"Answer the question, Alfhild," Grigor instructed me from his seat. "Ilya can ask whatever she wants. This is the court of Castle Iadului and you are under The Vampire Nation here. What did you think of Thaddeus?"

I glared at him. "Perhaps what's more important is what *you* thought of him. He was *your* son after all." I raised my chin in a direct challenge. "But a little bird told me that you hadn't had much to do with him in decades."

Grigor leaned forward on his throne and growled at me. "Did they? He *was* my son. Yes. My second son. And you killed him. That's why you're the one on trial here."

"Would you even care if your eldest son was not also missing and presumed dead?" I shot back.

Grigor's eyes flashed with hatred and he nodded at the shadow guard standing behind me. A slap landed on the side of my head, hard enough to make my teeth rattle.

"You killed him, and you will pay, Alfhild," the prince snarled.

My eyes smarted as I glowered at him, hardly comprehending what I was hearing. "If you already believe that I killed him, then why are we even going through with this farce?"

"Answer the question!" he thundered, showering me with spittle.

With my hands bound I couldn't wipe his spit from my face. I knelt there, helpless. What could I do, but answer his questions, as loaded as they were? "I didn't think anything of him initially. All of them... the vampires... they were a handful. He... Thaddeus..." I tried to remember him. Dashing. Young. Full of energy. "Handsome. I remember that."

Giggles from the crowd in the shadows.

"And like everyone who turned up that night, almost without exception," I continued, thinking of Marc Williams and how sweet he had always been, "they were a complete pain in my backside."

"Interesting," Ilya made a note. "Would you care to elucidate?"

I recalled the mess I'd woken up to those first few mornings the vampires had stayed with me. The broken glass and wine stains on the walls. The amount of alcohol they had managed to get through. "Put it this way, their capacity to party was like nothing I'd ever experienced before. And, believe me, as someone who had worked in hospitality all her adult life, that was going some."

There were whistles from the shadows. Of course I couldn't expect sympathy from anyone in this hall, but the way Melchior and his posse had treated Charity and my ghosts at the time had been an outrage.

"And so Thaddeus was, as you claimed and I quote, a pain in the backside?"

I nodded, stubbornly standing my ground, or kneeling, seeing as they wouldn't let me stand up. "Yes. Perhaps he wasn't as bad as one or two of the others, but certainly a part of all that went on. The carousing and noise, bothering the villagers where I live. It wasn't on."

"And so when the chance came to teach Thaddeus a lesson, you took it?"

I stared at Ilya in astonishment. She'd taken a huge jump, from me saying Thaddeus was badly-behaved to me killing him. "No," I shot out a flat denial for her ridiculous assertion.

"I put it to you, Miss Daemonne that you waited until all the other vampires had returned to the beer cellar and you incapacitated him in some way?"

"No."

"Come, come. You've admitted he was a thorn in your side."

"I didn't kill him."

"But you wanted him dead?"

I rolled my eyes. "As far as I'm concerned vampires are already dead. Half alive, half dead. Undead. Whatever. I didn't want him dead, but I'd have settled for him gone."

"Gone, dead. It's all the same to you, isn't it, Miss Daemonne?"

"I wanted Thaddeus gone from the inn the way I wanted all of the vampires gone from the inn. I made a mistake agreeing to host the wedding in the first place. I should have listened to my great-grandmother."

There was a commotion behind me, whispers and curses.

"Ah yes," hissed Prince Grigor. "Alfhild Daemonne the first."

Angry murmurs from the shadows. I half turned and received a timely prod between my shoulder blades. The vampires were reacting to Gwyn's name.

"You're so like her," the prince was saying, and he sounded almost sad. "But unlike her, I'm afraid you won't escape our justice."

What justice had he wanted to exact on my great-grandmother? My mind raced. Gwyn had never told me anything about her experience with the vampires. Thank the goddess she had escaped whatever fate had befallen her companions here in 1924.

The Prince shifted in his seat and whined, "Do let's get this over with, Ilya."

"Of course, my prince." Ilya bowed to him and turned to me. "We've established that you wanted Thaddeus dead—"

"We've established no such thing," I snapped back at her.

"You had means, motive and opportunity, did you not?"

"I'd gone up to bed. As far as I was concerned my guests would be back in their coffins when I awoke."

"Can you tell us what happened when you came downstairs?"

I thought back. "The lights wouldn't work. I called for Zephaniah, one of the ghosts who works for me—"

"So he fixed the fuse?"

"No. He never turned up. Not in time. Ch—" I stopped. I couldn't give Charity away. She'd been the one to open the curtains, but she hadn't known that Thaddeus had been tied to the chair.

"Zephaniah is a ghost?" Titters from the edges of the room.

"Yes. He fixes things around the inn."

"Not that morning though?"

I shook my head. If I could have changed anything it might have been that we'd waited for Zephaniah to arrive.

"Somebody set me up," I said, more quietly. "Someone else tied Thaddeus to that chair, knowing that opening the curtains was the quickest and easiest way for us to light up the room when we discovered that the lights had failed. We wouldn't have thought twice about it. It's a perfectly natural thing to do in the morning." I sniffed. "Well it is if you're a mortal."

Growls from the shadows. They sounded more and more like a pack of hungry dogs. I swallowed. "I'm telling you, I was set up," I repeated.

Ilya shook her head, her face incredulous. "Unfortunately there were no other suspects, Miss Daemonne. It is my supposition that given enough time, your hatred of vampires was such that you might have picked them off one by one." Ilya turned triumphantly to Prince Grigor. "That is the case as the Nation sees it, my Prince. I have tendered the facts. It is now for you to proffer sentence."

"This is preposterous," I said, trying to twist my hands free from their bonds and glaring at Grigor once more. "I need to speak to Wizard Shadowmender. You are obliged to let me talk with him."

I didn't see him move, but he did, fast as lightning.

Prince Grigor leapt to his feet and jumped from the dais, landing lightly to my side. The unexpected fluidity of his movement jarred my senses. The soft patter of his feet was one of the most chilling sounds I'd ever heard. They slapped on the ground as he ran for me, but I had no time to process the sound before he'd clamped his leathery hands around my neck. He twisted my head painfully, upwards and to the left, baring my throat to the light, then dug one of his claw-like nails into the skin close to my jugular.

Inhaling slowly, the air hissing as it passed over his ancient vocal cords, he brought his face level with mine. I gagged at the stench of him, unable to avoid the stink of earth and ripe meat and rancid milk. His tongue ran the length of my jaw and up towards my mouth, sticky and slick. I tried to wrench my head away, but he gripped me more tightly until I feared he would puncture the skin at my throat. "You forget yourself, Alfhild."

My insides turned to liquid and I understood what terror truly was. My windpipe clamped shut so I couldn't breathe, and even my heart seemed to pause, hanging painfully mid-beat, awaiting certain death.

My eyes rolled in their sockets, watching this monster, while my brain wanted to shut down my senses, to escape the horror. Always in times of trouble, I'd called on my inner reserves of strength and waited for the right opportunity to strike back. I'd tried to be proactive, to be strong, but here I was, in chains, on the floor of The Great Hall of a remote castle in Transylvania, in the middle of a vampire nest, with the hands of an angry vampire wrapped around my neck.

And he wanted vengeance.

I felt liquid trickle down the side of my neck. Blood. My blood. He'd punctured the skin. My fevered imagination ran riot. Those that haunted the shadows, they were waiting for this moment. They would all fall on me now, surround me like starving sharks. They would rip me to shreds.

I closed my eyes. *Silvan!* I sent out the thought as loudly as I could. *Help me now.*

As suddenly as he'd attacked me, he threw me down. I lay on my side, breathing heavily, watching him as he licked my blood from his fingernail with evident glee. "You killed my son and you will pay. But not here. Later tonight. At midnight. We'll make a meal of it."

He laughed. The ultimate sadistic peel of evil. The sound chilled my soul.

He threw his arms wide, addressing the occupants of The Great Hall in their entirety. "I pronounce Alfhild Daemonne guilty of the wilful destruction of my son Thaddeus Corinthian. The penalty is—"

He leaned down towards me, his grotesque body contorted in excitement. "Death."

The room exploded with approving cheers and vicious shrieks.

I struggled to right myself, attempting to make myself heard above the din, my quaking voice hoarse with fear. "That wasn't a fair trial. I demand to be heard! Ambassador Rubenscarfe?"

The ambassador scuttled backwards, away from me. *You shallow and treacherous monster*, I screeched inwardly.

I cried after him, "You have to talk to Wizard Shadowmender. He needs to hear of this." The ambassador stared at me blankly, as though he had no idea who I was or what my connection to him might be.

"Ambassador?" I tried again. "The Ministry of Witches will not look favourably upon this. I demand my own counsel—"

"Oh shush now, Alfhild! You and your demands!" Grigor sounded positively cheery. "But perhaps you're right. Perhaps I should find someone who can help you. Hmmmm." He made a great show of looking around the room. Some of his followers edged out of the shadows, waving at him and laughing. "Are there any volunteers in here who would care to assist Miss Daemonne?"

He stalked along the row of shadow guards

behind me, peering closely at each masked face. My stomach, already quivering with distress, sank into my knees. "Anybody at all who would like to help Miss Daemonne out on this occasion? Perhaps explain her side of the story?"

He came to the end of the row of guards and snapped back towards me, his eyes deep wells of hatred.

"No. There isn't. And do you know why there isn't?" In my peripheral vision I spotted Nadia as she motioned at the two men guarding the entrance to the hall. They heaved the huge doors open.

"Because we took your treacherous friend into custody earlier." Grigor nodded at Nadia and she beckoned somebody outside.

"Bring him in," she called.

A pair of hefty shadow guards dragged a man in between them. They gripped him tightly under the armpits. His head lolled lifelessly, his legs dragging behind him.

Silvan.

They threw him at my feet, and he collapsed there, not moving at all. I gazed down in horror at his broken body. His swollen eyes and lips and broken nose.

A scream began to build inside me. It was all my

fault we'd ended up here. If I had turned down the invitation to host the wedding at Whittle Inn the previous Halloween as Gwyn had wanted me to do, none of this would have happened.

Had I done this?

Had I killed Silvan?

CHAPTER THIRTEEN

It appeared the nest needed time to prepare The Great Hall for the proceedings required to carry out my sentence at midnight. For that reason they escorted me back upstairs to my room. A pair of shadow guards half-dragged half-carried Silvan in my wake and threw him down on the floor as soon as we were inside.

Guards were posted outside the door in order, no doubt, to ensure that I didn't get up to any of my previous tricks and go walkabout. Not that I imagined I'd make it very far now that night had fallen and every vampire in the castle was awake and preparing for the banquet of the year. It looked like Silvan and I were lined up as the main course.

As the door slammed closed and the locks were jammed into position I took in the devastation of the room. The whole place had been turned upside down, the bed stripped, the wardrobe and cupboards emptied. What few belongings I had brought with me were scattered over the floor. Maybe they'd been after my mobile phone or my wand. It didn't matter.

I fell to my knees beside Silvan, hardly daring to touch him, but when I did reach out to search for a pulse, his eyelids fluttered, and he looked up me through rapidly swelling lids.

I caught my breath and without thinking wrapped my arms around his neck, cradling him against me. "Thank the goddess. Thank the goddess," I cried. He moaned. I could feel his body shaking so I eased his head back to the floor.

"Can you hear me?" I asked, my tears dropping onto his face as I bent close to listen for a response.

He groaned. "Of course I can hear you." His voice sounded choked, frail. Evidently in pain, he made an attempt at a joke. "There's nothing wrong with my ears."

"Good," I tried to laugh but sobbed instead. "Where does it hurt?"

He struggled as though he would sit up, so I pressed him back down. "It hurts pretty much everywhere." He lifted his hands into the space between us and I stared in horror. "Especially my hands."

Broken fingers.

"They did this to you?" I whispered, my voice almost lost in despair, my breath catching in my throat. I stroked his head with my own shaking hands. "We'll make them pay for this. I promise." I glanced up at the door, my eyes boring through the wood, searching for the whereabouts of Grigor. If I'd had a wooden stake to hand...

"They weren't very happy to find out they had a spy in their midst."

I clamped my hands to my mouth. *All my fault!* That's all I could think. If I hadn't foolishly trusted Ambassador Rubenscarfe then Silvan's existence would have remained a secret. "What have I done?" I moaned.

"It wasn't you."

"It was! I told the ambassador—"

"Alf! Stop!" Silvan tried to reach for me, but he recoiled as his hands made contact with me. "It's not what you've done or said that matters now." He tried to sit up again but moaned at the pain. "What does matter is what we're going to do next." I tried to restrain him once more, but he waved me away. "Time's passing. We will not die here," he said.

His earnestness broke through the fury of my own emotions. He had a point. We couldn't just wait for Grigor to send up for us. We would not wait here, patient for our own deaths.

We had no choice but to choose to fight. I helped Silvan to his feet. He leaned heavily on me as I led him towards the bathroom. "Come on," I said. "Let's get you cleaned up."

Archibald hovered around us, his face glum, as I wound torn up strips of my bed sheet around Silvan's fingers, binding the broken ones to their neighbours, in an effort to temporarily stabilise his injuries. I'd gingerly wrapped thicker strips of sheet around Silvan's chest, hoping this would have the same effect for his ribs.

Oh how I wished I knew more about medicinal magicks. If only I could conjure Millicent to help. Or even simply ring her and ask her advice, but of course, even supposing I'd found a signal, my phone had been lost. I wondered if any of the shadow guards had stumbled across it during their sentry duty on the roof. Was it now in the possession of Grigor?

I'd cleaned Silvan up, but his swollen eyes, and

his pale face told me he was suffering. I scrabbled around on the floor among my spilled possessions and located the mundane packet of painkillers I always kept in my bag for emergencies. I offered him three with a glass of water.

"We have to get out of here somehow," he said, swallowing the horse-sized tablets with a grimace.

I glanced at the door, knowing full well that the shadow guards would put a quick end to any escape plan I could hatch.

And yet...

Gwyn had escaped from the castle. There had to be a way.

I rolled my head back and stared at the ceiling, thinking. Thinking hard. I could only wish I'd interrogated my great-grandmother more about her hatred of vampires. If I had, then maybe she would have told me about her experiences in Transylvania. I might have heard about her great and daring escape—I would have been able to learn from her experience. She wasn't the kind to brag of such things, but escape she had.

On many occasions people had likened me to her. If she could do it, I could do it.

"There has to be another way out of here." I

stood and marched with purpose to the door. Silvan, slumped on the edge of the bed, turned his head with difficulty and watched me through his swollen eyelids.

"There isn't," Archibald argued.

I yanked at one of the tapestries, pulling it as hard as I could so that it fell away from the wall. Nothing behind it but stained plaster.

"I can assure you there really isn't," Archibald said again as I repeated the process with the next tapestry. It made a flumping sound as it hit the floor.

"There must be!" Furious now, I tugged and tugged again at the next one. Thicker, heavier. My nails snagged and broke, but I didn't care. It finally dropped to the floor and dust billowed out around me, coating the thin sheen of perspiration on my face in grit.

"Grandmama made it out of this castle alive and so will we." I mashed my teeth together in desperation and paced round and round the room, looking for something, anything, some way out. There were only the plastered walls, the heavy locked door, the bathroom, and the narrow stain-glassed windows.

I shook my head in annoyance and spun about again.

Walls. Door. Bathroom. Windows.

Walls. Door. Bathroom. Windows.

Walls. Door. Bathroom—

The windows.

Archibald noticed my sudden interest in the windows set on either side of the burning fire.

"Madam, I wouldn't even consider those as an exit strategy."

"Why not?" I demanded and marched over to them, trying the handle of the one on the right. It wouldn't budge. I wasn't sure whether the frames had simply seized up after years of not being used or whether they had been locked to prevent anyone escaping. Either way, I wasn't intending to let a stupid inconvenience like a window lock hold me back.

"We're a long way up, Madam. A very long way."

"Well what's the alternative?" I muttered and fished my wand out of my bodice. From the direction of the bed came a snort. I elected to believe that Silvan was brim full of admiration for my perspicacity in the face of adversity. I tapped the window lightly with the tip of my wand. "*Reserare,*" then slid the wand along a little way and repeated the process. "*Reserare.*" Round and round the outside edge of the window frame I went until finally, when I tried the handle for the umpteenth time, it gave a little. With brute force I shoved it open.

The wind instantly rushed into the room, biting with cold. I shot a wary look at the door, wondering whether the shadow guards would notice the freezing draft escaping underneath it. I needed to offset that chance, so I grabbed one of the heavy tapestries and did my best to ball it up before carefully pushing it against the door as quietly as possible to use as a draught-excluder. I didn't intend to alert the guards to what I was up to.

Wiping my hands on my robes, I made my way back to the window. It was slightly too high for me to lean out, so I grabbed a chair from the dining set and placed it against the wall in front of the window.

Archibald fluttered around me in consternation. "Really, Madam—"

"Hush Colonel Peters. I need to think," I warned him, seriously considering sending the spirit back to where he had come from. I took a deep breath and climbed onto the chair then stuck my head outside.

"Ooooh." I wobbled on the chair, my head swimming. It was every bit as bad as bad as Archibald had warned. The good news was that this side of the castle did not face out into the courtyard. The bad news was that meant the drop was even more formidable. I can't tell you how high up we were. The grey stone walls of the castle appeared to merge into the rocky edifice of the hill the castle had been built upon. The valley tumbled away well below us. If I were hazarding a guess I'd say we were looking at a sheer drop of over two hundred feet. I drew back into the room and took a terrified breath.

"What can you see?" Silvan asked, struggling to stand.

"Stay there," I snapped at him, rubbing my forehead with a shaking hand. "Give me a minute."

I girded myself and leaned out again, further this time. I spotted a ledge around four feet below the window. Not particularly wide. Maybe twelve or fourteen inches. It ran all the way to the corner and disappeared around the side of the castle.

I'd seen those old films. Buster Keaton. The Bourne films. Hell, even more recently Tom Cruise had performed a spectacular getaway in one of the Mission Impossible films.

What if I could channel my inner Tom Cruise? He'd made it look easy.

Without taking time to think it through, I clambered onto the window ledge, severely hampered by my long skirt. The world seemed to tilt on its axis.

You're not afraid of heights, I told myself. *This is nothing.*

I could climb out and down onto the ledge, then ease myself around the corner. Maybe get in through a different window. Or perhaps climb up to the roof. Or maybe there would be a fire escape? Yes!

A medieval fire escape? What was I thinking?

And what? I'd just leave a severely injured Silvan behind me. Leave him to fend for himself? How long would he survive the next beating? Especially once the vampires noticed my disappearance. They would throw the book at him. They'd begin by eliciting information about my whereabouts. Demand answers. Take them by force.

I climbed down from the ledge. Silvan gazed up at me from his spot on the bed, although how much he could actually see through his swollen eyelids I wasn't entirely sure. Looking at his battered face made me want to weep again. Differing emotions battled for dominance inside me.

I looked from him to the locked door. I couldn't leave him here alone. He deserved better that that.

"What time is it?" I asked.

Archibald consulted his pocket fob, and that action momentarily reminded me of Mr Wylie and his Gimcrack. How I wished I had a Gimcrack to hand right now. "It's 10.36," he told me.

No time to lose. Prince Grigor wanted to start his hellish ceremony at midnight. That meant Nadia and the guards would come for us within an hour or so. Scouting around I found my robes. They'd been kicked under the bed among my other belongings. I yanked at my dress, tearing it from my body and quickly pulled my robes on, then located my cloak. Silvan, still wearing his shadow guard black tunic and trousers, had no cloak. It would be cold outside. I threw mine over him.

"Do you have your wand?" I asked him as I carefully pocketed mine.

He shook his head. "They took it from me." That stood to reason. Neither Silvan nor I necessarily needed a wand but using one directed intent beautifully, thereby increasing a spell's power and efficacy. "It doesn't matter," I reassured him and helped him to stand.

"Madam," Archibald started. "I really don't think this is a good idea."

"So you've said. Unfortunately it's the only idea," I reminded him. "Now Colonel Peters, I don't expect your help, but I would be obliged to you if you never let on—"

"You can't think of leaving me here?" The Colonel ejected in dismay.

I stared him. "What do you mean? Are you saying you want to come with us?"

"I'd rather not remain another minute with these monsters." He glided over to the window. "I've done my time at Castle Iadului."

I shooed him out the way as I guided Silvan across to the chair. "Of course you can come. But don't get your hopes up. We may be joining you in the after world sooner rather than later. I wouldn't get too comfortable with the notion we'll be free of this place any time in the immediate future."

"There's nothing like putting a positive spin on things, is there Alfhild?" Silvan mumbled, and I did a double take. For a minute there, he'd sounded for all the world like my great-grandmother.

"Listen to me, Silvan." I waved my hand close to his swollen eyes and he flinched. Good. He had some vision. "I don't know whether this will work or not. It's not the most sensible thing I've ever done but I need you to do everything I say. And I mean follow every single instruction I give you. Immediately and without question." For once his face remained serious and he didn't try to tease me or lighten the mood.

"This is the only way?" he asked.

I kept a tight lid on my own fear. "Yes," I replied; my voice deadly serious. "You're going to have to trust me." I turned around so my back was towards him, then reached behind for his hands, placing them on my hips. "Follow me," I told him.

"To the ends of the earth," he replied.

CHAPTER FOURTEEN

What a sight we'd have made, if anyone could have actually seen us. Fortunately I couldn't envision that being a problem as we headed outside onto the ledge, to cling on for dear life, on a dark and cold Autumn night. This side of the castle wasn't overlooked so you'd have needed to be on the ground in the forest with a strong pair of binoculars and known to look for us in order to see us. And even then we'd have looked like ants on a wall probably.

Throwing my leg out and over the sill was the hardest part.

No. That's a lie.

It was the first of the hard parts. Each action, each movement I took, every decision I made, was as excruciating as the last.

The wind snapped at the skirts of my robes as I gingerly turned myself about on the window ledge, but I quickly worked out that the prevailing wind was coming at us. This was fortunate as it served to push me back against the wall. I felt reassured having Silvan's hands on me, although I was sure there was no way he'd be able to hold onto me if I should happen to slip, given the state of his broken fingers. He released me, and with my heart hammering like a drill in my chest, I let myself drop down to the ledge. When first one foot and then the next found purchase I allowed myself a relieved, although shaky, breath.

I inched along the ledge to make room for Silvan. "Okay," I told him. "It's fine. Climb on to the window ledge and turn yourself about. You need to come down backwards. Keep close to the wall and whatever you do, don't let go."

"Genius," I heard him mutter as he manoeuvred himself around with difficulty.

"Take it easy," I said in alarm as he wavered.

"Stop worrying," he called back to me and slid down to join me, grimacing as he gripped at the ledge.

"Okay, Colonel Peters," I called. "Your turn."

Of course it was far easier for him, he simply floated out of the window and hovered on the ledge beside Silvan.

"My goodness. It's a long way down." Archibald tilted his whole body and stared into the dark valley.

"That's not helpful, Colonel." I swallowed a wave of nausea.

"You'd be able to sing the first verse *and* a chorus of God Save the Queen on your way down there," Archibald, continued, undaunted.

"Colonel!" I snapped.

Silvan shivered beside me.

"That's the trickiest bit done," I lied. "Now we need to make our way over to the corner."

Archibald interrupted me. "Might I make a suggestion, Madam?"

"I suppose so," I said, a tad irritably. Now we were out of the castle and risking our lives I just wanted to get on with it. "Shoot."

"We should seal the window up again. That will confuse them."

Why hadn't I thought of that? "That's a great idea, Colonel," I enthused. "If you two could squidge along a little, I'll do that."

Silvan edged sideways, to allow me to stand in front of the window once more. I pushed it closed as hard as I could, praying that the shadow guards standing in front of the door wouldn't hear the commotion, then pulled my wand out of my pocket.

Carefully I retraced the magick I'd performed earlier. "*Hoc claudere stricta. Adhæsit hic erit,*" I repeated my mantra over and over again, weaving threads of unbreakable magick from the tip of my wand. The only problem being that I couldn't reach the top of the window now that I stood four feet below on the ledge.

Not to worry. I'd done my best.

"Okay." I breathed noisily, pocketing my wand once more. "Let's go."

What I hadn't taken into consideration were the lack of hand holds.

This wasn't really a problem to begin with because we could hang on to the window ledges. There'd been two windows in my room, and the room next door to me—evidently the corner suite—also had two. At any one time, either Silvan or I were able to hold on to a ledge while supporting each other—we did this by hooking elbows so as to alleviate the strain on poor Silvan's fingers. But after we'd passed the final pair of windows there was a longer expanse of wall with no holds at all.

I worried about this as we edged slowly

onwards. Every foot of area we covered seemed to take us an age. Occasionally I glanced back at the window we'd climbed out of, expecting to spot someone emerging after us at any minute, ready to give chase.

We were running out of time. We needed to move more quickly. And yet the section of wall without handholds loomed large in our future.

I paused once we were all safely under the final window.

"Problem?" Silvan asked, and I could hear the strain in his voice. I couldn't begin to imagine how much pain he was in.

I leaned my shoulder gently against his, attempting reassurance. "Nothing a parachute wouldn't help with," I joked.

"I think they confiscated mine along with my wand," he returned.

"Hmm. That does cause us a small problem then." I blew my cheeks out and examined the wall. The castle had been made with hand cut blocks of stone centuries before, but the surface appeared remarkably flat. Quite an achievement. I rubbed the palm of my hand out in front of me. I could just make out the join, and in places weeds and grass grew out of the minutest of ledges.

"What would Tom do?" I asked aloud, more to myself than anyone else.

"Tom who?" asked Silvan.

"Cruise."

Colonel Peters, on the other side of Silvan, looked bemused by the turn the conversation had taken

"You mean Tom Cruise the actor?" Silvan asked.

"I mean Tom Cruise the actor who does all his own stunts, including parachuting and rock climbing."

Silvan snorted gently. "Yes, but still has a team of safety experts on hand, just in case."

"We could do with that sort of team."

"And he puts in hours and hours *and hours* of training," Silvan reminded me. "We haven't. Is that the Tom Cruise you mean?"

"That's the one." I had a quick giggle at the absurdity of two witches and a ghost huddled together on the ledge of an old castle trying to emulate a movie actor. "Sadly I forgot to attend the castle wall climbing workshop the last time it ran."

"Me too." Silvan shivered in the cold while I considered our options.

Finally I broke the silence. "In that film with the big glass building he has a sticky glove."

Silvan nodded, remembering. "He climbed the Burj Khalifa, that's right."

With a sudden realisation I gripped Silvan's upper arm. "Could we do that?"

Silvan's brain worked as quickly as mine. "That was glass. This is stone."

"But is there a spell that would work?" I asked.

Silvan considered this for a moment. "I'm not sure anyone has ever had need of one. We'd have to adapt one. We could try the sticky spell."

I'd used a sticky spell in the past. I was dubious about its strength to stick us to rock, but we were rapidly running out of time.

"Give me a time check, please, Colonel."

The ghost plucked out his watch fob and narrowed his eyes in the dim light. "Eleven sixteen, Madam."

"Already?" My heart lurched. We didn't have a choice.

Sticky it would have to be.

"If we both say it together?" I asked Silvan and he nodded. "We can make it stronger."

"Intent is everything, Alfhild. You know that."

"Well I certainly intend to hang onto this rock for dear life," I told him. "Are you ready?"

"Ready."

I lay the palms of my hands flat against the rock surface in front of me, then focused hard on both hands at once—not easy to do. I willed them to push into the face of the wall, be as one with the rock. "Three. Two. One." A flash of energy lit up the air around us. "*Tenax!*"

Something shifted beneath my hands. I wobbled, thinking I might fall. My stomach lurched queasily. But when I tried to release my hand from the window ledge I found I couldn't detach it at all. Momentarily I panicked, but beside me Silvan exhaled softly, and I heard an amused grunt.

"You see the power of the magick we can create when we work together?" he asked, and I couldn't disagree. With him by my side, I always felt I could overcome the odds. "You'll need to focus to release each hand," he continued. "Think of it as a snapping action."

I recalled the way Tom Cruise had peeled each hand away from the wall in a rolling motion, before some kind of magnetism had snatched each hand back. Effective until he'd lost one of the gloves.

Eww. I hadn't needed to remind myself of that.

I didn't intend to lose a hand though.

There could be no practicing. I was in the lead therefore I had to play the part of Guinea pig. I rolled my hand away from the castle wall and took a step before slapping my palm back against the surface. It clung there the way a barnacle clings to the bottom of a boat.

"It works!" I laughed in delight.

Above us, a light went on the window. Somebody had entered the room.

We froze. Had the shadow guards discovered our absence? Had they started to search?

We pressed into the wall, hardly daring to breathe, but we couldn't stay there. The likelihood of someone thinking to check was too high. We had to keep moving and navigate the corner.

"Come on," I whispered. "Let's keep going."

I'm not sure why, when I originally climbed out of the bedroom window, I decided to head right. I think it was the closest corner, so it made sense to get out of sight. However, once we made it to the corner we encountered a new problem. Castle Iadului was enormous. And now as I poked my head around the edge of the wall, the new side of it—as far as I could tell given the lateness of the hour and the lack of light—seemed to go on for miles and miles.

In addition to that, we would now be heading into the wind. It stung my eyes as I blinked into the distance.

I edged around the corner, focussing fully on my hands.

Roll and slap. Roll and slap. Roll and slap.

Once I'd safely manoeuvred my way around—and had a measure of the full force of the wind—I peeled one hand away and held tight to Silvan's elbow as he edged round to join me.

"Careful," I said, glad that my body would shield him from the worst of the strong current of air. "It's a little breezy this side."

"We've got this," he replied, his tone chipper, but I could see the strain etched on his pale face.

I glanced down the length of castle wall once more finding dozens of sets of windows, some of them burning brightly. Silvan must have followed my gaze.

"Do we have a plan yet?" he asked.

That would be a no.

"What time is it?" I asked Archibald again.

"Eleven forty-eight, Madam."

I bit my lip. They had to know we were missing by now. Or if they didn't, they soon would.

"Let's press on," I said, more confidently than I felt. I led them forwards, fighting against the wind the whole time. Inch by inch we moved. My toes numb as they pressed into the ledge, for the most part my face hovered just centimetres from the rough surface of the castle's walls. Every time I relinquished a hand hold my stomach would flutter with nerves.

Roll and slap. Roll and slap.

Whatever else I did, I refused to look down into the vast crevice behind me. I found myself almost envying Silvan his semi-blind state. Occasionally I would feel him falter next to me, and I would pause. Knowing he would become irritated if I kept asking him how he was, I would instead assure him we were making good progress.

But that progress seemed dangerously slow to me.

One particularly vicious gust of wind came out of nowhere and for a moment I pushed back against Silvan. His sharp intake of breath alerted me to his discomfort, and I paused once more, allowing us time to take a breath and refocus.

"We can do this." I spoke aloud the mantra I'd been silently repeating for what seemed like hours.

"It may be the craziest thing I've ever done," Silvan volunteered, wincing as he straightened his back. "And I thought time-travel was up there."

"Is there anything I can do to help you?" I asked.

"Or me, good Sir?" Archibald asked from behind him.

Silvan shook his head slowly. "You're doing—both doing—a great job."

On occasion, lights appeared in windows above us and every time they did my nerve would falter. They must have been searching the whole castle for us by now, imagining that somehow we had slipped past the guards. If I had been them I'd have started with the bedrooms. How long would it take them to cotton on to the fact that the locked window was a ruse?

I could imagine the furore rapidly followed by Prince Grigor's fury. His wrath would be pretty devastating if we were caught.

So it made sense not to be.

I set my jaw and we continued to creep forwards. Above us, the waxing moon shone down on us but only intermittently. Clouds moved speedily across the sky, driven by the easterly wind. Occasionally we were plunged into near darkness, but it rarely lasted long, and holding onto the wall for dear life as we were, we were hardly going to take a wrong turning.

When we rested once more, I glanced back at Archibald. He didn't even have to wait for me to ask. "Twelve thirty-two, Madam."

My soul lifted momentarily. We were passed the witching hour, and nobody had located us thus far.

"So far, so good," Silvan said.

But for how long? This side of the castle seemed endless. We couldn't carry on circumnavigating the castle endlessly. At some stage we would have to find a way to get down or get off the ledge. I had imagined that we would climb in through a window and hide out in a bedroom, but every time I spotted light streaming from a window above my head, I realised this was not such a good idea.

I rested my head against the wall in front of me, suddenly feeling infinitely weary.

"We can do this," Silvan reminded me. "Remember?" I turned my face away so that he couldn't catch a glimpse of my despair slowly starting to build. At least up ahead the middle expanse of this side of the castle appeared devoid of the little windows. It had become tiring trying to dodge them every few metres, always fearing someone would open one and find us.

Devoid of *most* windows...

The exception was a much larger one.

It had to have been some sort of late addition, I imagined. A balcony jutted out from the edifice, supported by solid wooden struts. As we approached it my knees quaked. This would be a tough obstacle to navigate even for me, and I had all my faculties. I trembled at the thought of trying to help Silvan through this and out the other side.

The night stretched endlessly ahead, along with thoughts of our impending doom given the challenges we had to surmount. An enormous lump lodged in my throat.

I mentally shook myself, annoyed that I threatened to give in to my emotions. *We can do this!*

"Alright, Alf?" Silvan asked beside me, perhaps sensing the maelstrom of emotions I was fighting. I swallowed and recalibrated my thoughts.

The night wasn't endless. It would pass.

A light went on in the hidden recesses of my mind.

And when it passed the day would come. And the sun would rise. The vampires would go to bed. They had no choice. They couldn't operate in the daylight.

If we could bide our time until daybreak, we would get through this.

"Madam?" Archibald's voice cut into my excited thoughts.

"We need to press on," I said.

"Madam?" Archibald insisted.

I turned back to look at him. "What's up?"

He pointed into the sky and I followed the direction of his finger not seeing anything at first, but once I did I knew we had to redouble our efforts to move quickly.

Flitting across the three-quarter disc of the moon were small jagged shapes.

Bats.

The vampires were extending their search outside the confines of the castle.

CHAPTER FIFTEEN

I bit back a shriek.

The bats had exited the castle high above us, probably from the roof. With any luck they wouldn't spot us immediately, but we had to move quickly.

"What's the problem?" Silvan asked, looking about himself. His eyes were now so swollen, I doubted he could see much at all.

I leaned close to him and whispered in his ear. "Bats. No messing. We have to move quickly now. Not far. Another eight metres or so. As fast as we can. Okay?"

He nodded his assent and taking a deep breath I reached out a hand and moved my foot at the same time. The devil had me in his sights and it was time to double up my efforts.

Roll and slap. Roll and slap. As quickly as I could. No time to think. No time to breathe.

Hurry. Hurry. Hurry.

I glanced at the sky. One or two bats fluttered high above us but not with any sense of alarm. We were still safe. I didn't waste my breath to cajole the others, just kept on. Eight metres, seven metres. Six. Five. Four.

Silvan stopped.

I put my lips to his ear. "Not now. We have to keep going."

He shook his head, his breathing ragged.

"Four metres. That's all that's left, Silvan. Do it for me." I urged him on.

His shoulders sagged and he nodded. Roll and slap. Step. Roll and slap.

Three metres. Two.

The balcony jutted out above my head now, the struts blocking my way just a metre further in. But we could huddle under here and be sheltered from the vagaries of the weather, and unless the bats chose to look in every nook and crevice—which was a possibility I suppose—we would be blocked from their view.

I gripped the first strut and examined the underside of the balcony. To my surprise, I found a hollowed-out space behind it. The castle walls were thick, several metres in some cases, designed to withstand siege weapons such as a trebuchet or a mangonel.

Whoever had decided they needed a panoramic window here had made a space larger than required.

"There's a kind of cave here," I announced excitedly. My voice sounded strange now we were undercover, the wind no longer whipping my words away, but louder too. I lowered it. "We can hide out here till morning."

With difficulty I demonstrated to Silvan where he should go. We were cold and stiff as we climbed into the gap which normally would not have been overly difficult but had now became an almost insurmountable task. With Archibald's encouragement, soon enough, Silvan and I were huddled together in a gap measuring around twelve feet across by six feet deep and perhaps three feet in height. The walls of the cave, as I thought of it, were rough and unfinished, and the whole place was damp, but this was the most sacred of sanctuaries and I collapsed on the cold floor with heartfelt relief.

Silvan shivered. Now we had stopped we were going to feel the strain of our endeavours. I scooted across until I could lie next to him and wrapped my arms around him. "You're going to be fine," I said. "A few more hours. That's all."

"Is there a plan yet?" he whispered as he clumsily enveloped me in a bear hug.

That would still be a no.

We lay there together, sharing body heat while the Colonel flitted in and out and round about, keeping an eye on the bats, and occasionally creeping back along the ledge to see if anyone was hanging out of the windows. Or whether they had even been opened. If I'd have thought it would have been any use, I'd have sent him to fetch help, but so few people can actually see ghosts that I figured it would probably be a waste of time.

While we waited, Silvan drifted in and out of sleep. I welcomed his soft calm breathing and the relaxation of his body that went with it. When he awoke, he was once more wracked with the pain of his injuries, and he would become tense and quickly start to shiver. At those times I would hold him gently until he had weathered the worst and fallen into a doze once more.

For the most part I remained alert, my ears straining for the slightest sound. My mind was a movie screen of what I might be forced to do if they found us. I could push them off the rock face—as long as we weren't outnumbered—or I could invoke The Curse of Madb.

Once I might have quaked at the thought of that. I'd been taught that throwing hexes out like sweeties was never a good idea, and The Curse of Madb was particularly nasty. Invoked with the right amount of intent, it could pulverise the bones of the attacker and bring about instant death.

I'd never used it. Not even on The Mori.

But I would do anything to get us away from Castle Iadului and get Silvan to safety.

As if he could hear my thoughts, Silvan shivered next to me. His cloak had slipped, and I drew it together at his neck and wrapped my arms about him once more.

"What were you thinking about?" he murmured.

I smiled even though he couldn't see my face here in our dark crevice. "So many things." I stroked his back. "Mainly about the deep bubble bath I'm going to have when we get back home."

"Lots of suds?"

"Suds to the ceiling. Bergamot and rose scented. One of Millicent's specials." I luxuriated in the thought. "With an enormous mug of hot chocolate and marshmallows and a side helping of one of Florence's cakes."

"Which one though?"

"Which cake?" I ran though Florence's current obsessions. She tended to have fashions when it came to flavours. Hmm. Decisions, decisions. "She made a grand apricot and cardamom sponge last week, but I don't know. Coffee and pecan is one of my current favourites."

"Sounds good. I'd go for ginger and coriander."

What? "But you're a weirdo," I reminded him. "I'm really not sure coriander belongs in a cake."

Silvan laughed softly. "I may be weird, but you love me really."

He quietened again. I lay in the dark, listening to every painful breath he took. I was effectively alone. What were Silvan's chances of survival? How could I get us out? I ached with something I had never acknowledged before; an emotion I did not feel I could adequately express in words. This infuriating man, with his snark and his teasing…his jibes, felt like an aspect of myself I'd tried to hide my whole life. I often imagined he could see right through to the heart of me. He understood me—the way I thought, what I felt. And yes, he looked out for me even when I imagined he was being laissez faire or flippant. He'd been there every time I'd needed him from the moment we had first met.

Every. Single. Time.

Whenever he departed Whittle Inn to return to his business in Tumble Town he left me feeling bereft. There was no denying he was the yin to my yan, the gears in my engine, the frosting on my cupcake.

Quite simply he completed me.

But the words I yearned to say out loud were now stuck in my throat. I was going to fail him, and he didn't deserve that.

He reached up with his broken fingers, seeking my face and finding it, as he always did. He cupped my cheek, the makeshift bandages around his fingers rough against my skin. Purely by instinct he found a tear and wiped it away with his thumb.

"I love you, 'Alfie. You can do this. *We* can do this."

My heart melted. He loved me? He *really* loved me?

The darkest hour is just before dawn, apparently.

The night seemed never ending, but finally the

moon had sunk low, eventually disappearing below the horizon to the west. Even so, the sun seemed to be taking forever to peek its head up in the east.

I inched my way out towards the ledge and peered between the struts, seeking the faintest inkling of light.

Ice had settled in my veins and the wind bit. I wondered if I would ever warm up again. My sudsy bubble bath at Whittle Inn seemed a long way away. I turned west, focusing on my inn and the fires burning in the grates, sending feelings of love to my friends and the ghosts who awaited my return.

This yearning for home served as a useful reminder of why I needed to keep going. My fingers may have been numb, but the blood flowed through my veins with a new heat, and my heart soared with happiness. Silvan's declaration had boosted my spirits. I might have felt like a new woman but unfortunately every muscle in my body ached and my head was giddy with tiredness.

I sat at the edge of our hidey hole, waiting for the first rays of sunshine to creep above the forest canopy below while Silvan slept behind me, and tried to concoct a plan of action, but my mind kept wandering. Less than a week ago he and I had been playing with djinns in the garden, never imagining how quickly our lives would meet with this fresh disaster.

"I could do with a djinn, right now," I said aloud and then laughed. "A djinn *and* a gin." I thought about Zephaniah pouring me a gin and tonic and adding a slice of lemon at home. Remembered the blissful feeling of sinking into an overstuffed chair in front of the fire to enjoy it.

In my imagination I could see Gwyn there too... and Charity laughing with some of the guests... Finbarr leaning against the bar and asking Zephaniah to pour him a proper pint with a head, preferably of Guinness, while his pixies raced around the inn, plaguing the guests and stealing food from the kitchen.

The thought of Finbarr's pixies brought me back to conjuring djinns.

"Colonel?" I whispered and he appeared beside me immediately.

"I need you to stay here with Silvan. If he wakes up don't allow him to move."

"But Madam—"

"Not a muscle." I wagged a finger at Archibald. "I'll come back as soon as I can. And when I get here, I'll have help."

I rolled my shoulders up and backwards and stretched out as best I could, cricking my neck, kicking my legs and shaking my feet and hands. Every part of me had locked stiffly up in the four or so hours we had been sheltering in the cave. Clambering up to the balcony would have been difficult enough under normal circumstances, but here I was, cold to the bone and with a two-hundred-foot drop behind me.

Still, nothing ventured, nothing gained.

I slid out of the cave and tested my hands for stickiness. The spell held, so I dropped back down to the ledge and edged out into the open. At last I could see the first fingers of the new day finally appearing. My soul rejoiced at the sight and my blood felt a little less thin, my bones a little warmer. Prince Grigor and his nest of vengeful vampires had failed to find us, and we now had at least eight hours to get past the mortal guards and find a way to escape the castle.

A new day brought fresh optimism.

But I doubted we could do it on our own.

I took a firm hold of the end strut of the balcony

and, jamming my legs against the castle wall for leverage, began to scramble up the surface. Hand over hand I went, straining to climb up the wooden part of the under-balcony, until I could place one hand on the first stone lintel. The second hand followed and then it was a case of wriggling and hauling myself up with a brute strength that I'd never imagined I possessed. Once I had managed to jam a foot between the columns of the balcony, the rest was much easier. I tugged myself up until my belly was half over the low stone mantle, and then slithered down onto the floor with a plop, grazing my knees as I slipped.

Now on terra firma I allowed myself the luxury of sitting and taking a quiet moment to shake. Just for a few seconds. My body felt floppy, a combination of the extreme effort I'd been making and fear of falling.

But I'd done it.

I found myself on a balcony measuring perhaps twenty feet by eight feet. The pair of large arched doors here had an incredible vista. As far as the eye could see the forest stretched out below us, early morning mist rising above the tips of the trees, reaching for a sky rapidly taking on the colours of a bruised peach.

I stood and sucked in a lungful of morning air, grounding myself while considering my next move.

Slipping around the edge of the balcony, trying to remain out of sight from anyone inside who might glance out, I stood to one side of the first set of doors and slowly inched my head sideways to peer inside. I could see some sort of office or library. One of the castle's infamous permanently-burning fires lit the room. Books lined several shelves and an ornately carved desk stood in the middle of the room atop a large circular rug. A low couch and several easy chairs completed the room's furnishings.

Most importantly, the room was empty of people.

Perfect.

I tried turning the handle for the door and amazingly it swung open without fuss. I glared at the open door with distrust. Why make it that easy for me?

But thinking about it, I realised the door had been left unlocked because none of the inhabitants of the castle would expect anyone to break in from the balcony. Only a lunatic would try to access the room the way I had. I stifled a slightly hysterical giggle, reminding myself that every moment mattered. Silvan was still there, hiding in a hole in the wall under the balcony, and I had to get him out.

I glided inside and scanned my surroundings, beautifully clean and free of dust. A comfortable room, but it didn't appear that much was ever done here. Apart from the books on the shelves, there wasn't a great deal of clutter. No papers on the desk.

A number of portraits on the wall did grab my attention, however. They reminded me of the ones I'd hung in the bar at Whittle Inn of my great-grandmother and other ancestors, and I experienced another pang of longing for quiet days at my wonky inn.

I surveyed the paintings without a great deal of interest, until one in particular—the largest, hanging above the fireplace—called out to me. I studied it more closely, anxious to be getting on. It portrayed four men. One of them was sitting in a large carved throne-type chair, similar to the one in The Great Hall, the other three, younger, were grouped around him.

I stepped closer to the portrait. There could be no doubt that the man in the chair was Prince Grigor. Not as ancient looking perhaps, not quite as desiccated.

And the younger men? I recognised the tall one, a hand on his father's shoulder. Dark hair, black eyes. Thaddeus.

This was a family grouping. Grigor and his three sons. I didn't recognise one of the young men at all, he had to be the missing eldest son, but I realised with shock that I did know the other.

I clamped my hands to my mouth in surprise, wondering whether this meant anything or was a complete red herring.

I waved my hand at the picture, wishing I could somehow transmit the image to London. "Don't go anywhere," I told it. Its sheer size meant there could be no way to remove it from the wall and take it with me. I could cut it from the frame. I pondered on this, my stomach pulsing with nerves. Every second wasted delayed me finding help for Silvan. There was no time to stand and stare at the portrait, no time to try and cut if free. I had to get a move on and put part two of my plan into effect.

Deciding I'd return to the portrait later, I drew my wand out of my pocket and concentrated on a spot on the rug in front of the fire. Not so long ago, I'd been practising this spell with Silvan in the grounds of the inn, and I'd never managed to make it work. But maybe—just maybe—I hadn't put my heart and soul into it. Perhaps I'd been clowning around. Silvan often said so, after all.

Now, more than at any time, I needed this spell to work.

Pointing with the tip of the wand, I envisaged what I wanted, and then drew all my focus into my heart and the forefront of my mind. "*Parva venire magicis viventem!*"

A flash of blue light and a large puff of smoke, as fragrant as an autumn bonfire.

I wafted the smoke away and found myself face-to-face with a creature standing maybe twenty inches tall. To all intents and purposes he resembled a small muscular human with long black hair plaited in a tight rope down his back, but his skin was blue, quite a bright blue in fact, and he wore a robe of purple.

"Hello," I greeted him, hoping he spoke English.

He stared at me through mischievous brown eyes and remained mute.

"Isn't this where you're supposed to say, 'your wish is my command'?" I asked him. I'd seen the movies after all.

He cocked his head to one side, looked me up and down with evident disgust and pursed his lips. I decided that he obviously didn't speak my mother tongue. Silvan hadn't prepared me for this.

"My name is Alfhild," I pointed at myself,

speaking slowly and loudly. "And I need your help. If you don't mind. Please."

He sighed. "Why do I get all the amateurs?"

"Oh you do understand me?" I clapped in excitement.

"Of course I do." The djinn bore an expression of extreme weariness.

"Do you have a name?" I decided to try to coax some warmth out of him.

He drew himself up, angling his chin, his eyebrows—thick like a pair of furry caterpillars—set in a haughty arc. "My name, Mistress, is Paimon. I suppose I should be grateful that you have hauled me out of the dungeon of djinns; a rat infested and hateful hovel if ever there was one, but to be quite honest, I was enjoying a rest."

I nodded as though I understood to what he was referring, but I didn't have a clue. What did he mean by dungeon? Where on earth did he live?

He studied my face and tutted. "What is it with you witches? Have they added djinn-conjuring to the syllabus at the London academy or something?"

"No, I—"

He raised his right hand to study his nails. "Only, my last three conjurings have involved novice witches who haven't a clue what they're doing."

"I'm not a novice witch," I harrumphed in annoyance.

"You could have fooled me." He folded his arms with a wry shake of his head.

I glowered. "I'm not trying to fool you. But I do need your help rather desperately."

He raised his impressive eyebrows.

I needed to communicate the seriousness of our situation. I jabbed my finger back towards the arched door. "Out there is a dark witch who can run rings around your kind, and you'd better believe you'd be doing his bidding if it was him standing here and not me."

Paimon followed the direction of my finger, evidently seeing no-one on the balcony. He looked back at me rather warily.

"He's hiding out below the balcony. He's injured."

Paimon nodded. "I'd love to help but I'm no doctor."

"That's not what I need you to do for me."

Paimon walked over to the doors and stepped outside. "When you say below—"

"There's a kind of cutaway in the wall or the rock or whatever it is this castle has been carved out of. There's just enough space under there for the pair of us to lie flat. Which is what we've been doing for the past five hours, in fact."

"Ah." He nodded his understanding. "That's why you look like a charity shop reject."

The impudence. Of all the djinns I could have conjured how had I ended up with this insolent and bad-tempered creature?

"Listen—"

Paimon held a chubby hand up. "I can't carry him either. You'd need more than one djinn to help you with that. If he's as big as you, maybe you'd need an army of us."

"Do you mind?" I erupted.

He angled an enquiring eyebrow at me.

I remained silent for a minute, fighting my annoyance. If this little toad couldn't help me then I needed to send him back from where he'd come from. Paimon watched me, thinking, and perhaps he sensed he'd pushed me as far as he could because he suddenly dropped his puffed-up arrogance and turned a serious face upon me.

"Mistress?"

I regarded him in surprise, confused by the sudden change of tone. "Yes?"

"I sense someone heading our way." My stomach

dropped into my boots. He continued, "If it's true that you have spent half the night outside in order to avoid a confrontation, I suggest we make ourselves scarce."

"Where? Where?" I looked around in panic. There was a distinct lack of hiding spaces in this room.

"Under the desk, Mistress," Paimon suggested and without further ado dove there himself. The desk was one of those with an enclosed section at the rear, offering us the perfect hiding place. I hurriedly pulled the door to the balcony closed and dashed after the djinn, ducking under the top and squeezing myself in the well next to him. He lay flat on the rug, peeping out through the small gap between the bottom of the desk and the floor. Meanwhile I folded my legs so that every inch of me was tucked out of sight.

I held my breath as the door opened, clenching my muscles tight, scared that my clothes might rustle and give the game away. Whoever was at the door paused there for a second, muttered something to themselves, then walked slowly across the length of the room. I couldn't see them, but some of the light disappeared from the room so I could only imagine they were standing near one of the two doors, perhaps looking out at the balcony or the view beyond.

Or were they looking for us.

Just when I thought I would explode unless I started to breathe properly, the footsteps retreated back the way they had come. An internal door opened and closed, and I was alone again with the djinn.

We stared at each other in a newfound unity. This close I could smell his skin and hair. Vaguely musty—a damp dungeon in a place far away perhaps—but with an underlying tinge of some sort of incense and spice.

"Who was that?" I whispered.

"A rather large gentleman dressed in black with a mask," Paimon whispered back.

"They're still looking for us then. That's what I was afraid of." I stretched my cramped legs out. "Is the coast clear?"

Paimon concentrated, his eyes swivelling this way and that, and nodded. "There are others around but that one has headed away from here. Who are they?"

"They're called shadow guards. They're the mortal defenders of the owner of this castle." I winced as cramp set into my foot. "This castle belongs to a vampire and there's a whole nest of the vicious monsters asleep in various rooms. They're after my blood." I shuddered. "And everything else."

I shuffled out from under the desk and Paimon followed me. "You're in quite a bind, Mistress. This place is full of danger."

"I know." I pointed at the fire. "But I have a feeling that someone will be sympathetic to my plight." I smiled down at Paimon with what I hoped was a mixture of determination and encouragement. "Here's what I need you to do."

CHAPTER SIXTEEN

Paimon took the lead.

We crept out into the hallway and he moved swiftly and quietly ahead of me. I held my wand out ready to unlock a door should we need to swiftly locate a hiding place.

We moved with caution. Paimon's head turned this way and that as he scanned for more shadow guards. I had my eyes peeled but Paimon's senses were sharper than mine. Nothing was familiar so I wasn't sure in which direction to head, all I knew was that I wanted to get downstairs to the kitchen, and we needed to do it without eliciting unwanted attention.

This wasn't a part of the castle I had explored previously, but evidently this was where Prince Grigor resided. The rooms on this floor all had some sort of purpose, and we passed a few with open doors including a drawing room, and a smaller dining room for those days when you didn't fancy The Great Hall.

We made decent progress until suddenly Paimon pulled up, lifting his hand to warn me. He gestured urgently ahead of us. I tapped my wand against the lock of the nearest door. *"Reserare,"* I whispered and heard the welcome sound of rolling tumblers.

Quick as a flash I stepped in and Paimon followed me. I closed the door and leaned against it. I could clearly make out the sound of someone—even a pair of someones—walking down the hallway outside, heading straight for us. The room was dark, hardly a chink of light. I felt around, located what I imaged were tapestries and quickly hid myself behind them.

The footsteps halted in front of the door and I heard someone murmuring something unintelligible. The response was clear enough, however.

"That would be inconceivable."

I waited. Nothing more was said.

The footsteps started again and disappeared down the hallway.

Breathing a sigh of relief I fought my way out from behind the tapestry. Dust billowed around me, coating my face, and probably my lungs as I inhaled.

I waved it away from my face—entirely ineffectively—and, my eyes now growing more accustomed to the darkness of this room, made out a bed in the middle of the room.

Curiosity drove me forwards.

Lying in state on pillows of red velvet, his face as white as the driven snow, lay the ancient body of Prince Grigor. This was his bedroom. I stared down at his hateful visage. If I'd been a vampire hunter, or someone created in the mould of a Van-Helsing, maybe I'd have taken up a stake and plunged it through his unfeeling and slow beating heart.

But that's not who I was.

Even with Silvan hiding in abject pain outside, I couldn't lift my wand to finish him off.

I leaned over him, turning my nose up at his rancid stench. My heart thumped in my chest as I imagined him suddenly opening his eyes and sinking his razor-sharp fangs in the veins at my throat. Nonetheless, the beating of my own heart reminded me of how alive I was, and how I would fight to remain so.

I had a message for Grigor though. One he seemed intent on refusing to hear. "I didn't kill Thaddeus," I said, even though I assumed he couldn't hear me. "And blaming me for his death is never going to help you find the person who did."

I turned on my heel. "Let's get downstairs," I instructed Paimon and he nodded in agreement.

We exited the bedchamber and quietly closed the door, leaving Grigor to sleep the sleep of the wicked.

Like a pair of stealthy ninjas we continued on our way. Along hallways and down flights of stone stairs, avoiding main thoroughfares where possible. Occasionally we had further need to slip inside locked rooms, and always we found another vampire dead to the world on a bed. It appeared as if each of them was lying in state, and every single one we gazed upon seemed more beautiful and younger than the last.

Harmless at rest, I could only remind myself of the power these immortals wielded when awake. Deadly and frightening.

I remembered the rustling in the dark shadows of The Great Hall during my supposed trial. I could only imagine what devastation these beasts would have inflicted to me had I attended sentencing at midnight the previous evening, as Grigor had planned.

The kitchen was located in the basement, more or less positioned underneath The Great Hall. This must have been handy for when banquets of the more mundane variety were ordered. Paimon and I arrived at the hall via some grubby back stairs rather than the grand staircase. I cracked open the door and peered out. Someone—a caretaker of some kind—was pushing a broom around and whistling. The dais had been moved from the side of the room to what had effectively become centre stage, and I knew that had I been brought down here the previous evening, it would have been me who'd become the star attraction.

The whistling cleaner moved into view and I ducked back out of the way. An old man, he didn't look like he'd present much of a problem to us, but at this stage it seemed wise to take precautions. I knelt down so I could whisper in the djinn's ear.

"I need you to slip out and find a way down to the kitchen. Keep a good lookout for shadow guards, hide if you have to. Then come back."

He nodded and darted through the gap in the door, streaking past the old man with his broom. I remained on my knees, hunching close to the floor so I could watch the djinn without drawing attention to himself. The old man must have spotted movement out of his eye for he turned. Seeing nothing, for Paimon had ducked behind the dais, he carried on sweeping.

Paimon took stock of his surroundings. The main entrance was off to his right, the enormous fire in front of him. I watched him scan the walls and then head for something directly to the left of where I was hiding.

He disappeared from view and there was nothing I could do but wait.

I tried to remain calm despite the adrenaline pumping around my body. We were so close now. I could only ask the universe to give me a break. I waited an age but eventually I heard the soft sounds of Paimon's bare feet as he padded across the wooden floor of The Great Hall. The whistling had moved to the far corner. I eased the door open a little more and the djinn slipped to the floor beside me.

"Mistress, I have good news and bad news."

Isn't it always the way? "Go on."

"The woman you seek is below." That was good news indeed. "Unfortunately it also appears the shadow guards have their headquarters on the same floor and you're going to have to get past them in order to speak with her."

This was a disaster. "How many of them?"

"A dozen. Maybe more."

I rolled my eyes in exasperation. *That many?* I suppose in a castle this size, and given its many occupants, it wasn't entirely surprising. But what was I going to do? I couldn't kill them all. Couldn't send them into some endless sleep like their handlers...

I jolted at the thought.

Not an endless sleep... but a temporary one.

"Paimon?" He had poked his head back outside, keeping an eye on the caretaker. I tapped him excitedly on the shoulder. "I need you to dash upstairs and bring down a feather pillow. I've had a great idea."

Back in the days when I attended a witch school at weekends—before I thought I'd killed my father and decided I didn't want to be a witch any more thankyou-very-much—I'd been a fairly good student. One of my favourite spells—more hoax than hex—had been the slumber spell. My classmates were terrible for inflicting it on each other, resulting in one poor pre-selected victim falling asleep in class. Our teacher would be furious and produce their own wand to reawaken the victim, and would then be irritable for the rest of the lesson. I hadn't used the spell in a long while, and I'd only ever used it on individuals. Now I was going to try and cast it on at least a dozen people at once.

I carefully ripped open the pillow's seam, just a little, and gave it to Paimon to carry. Once the caretaker had his back to us, the djinn led me out into The Great Hall. Hugging the wall we flitted to the next door, with me mentally apologising to the caretaker for the trail of feathers we were leaving in our wake.

Once inside the stairwell, I noted that the walls were plain and the stairs twisty. I could smell the faint scents of roasted meat and vegetables. Plates of food had been carried up these stairs for centuries, used in a bid to tempt the appetites of unsuspecting guests who probably eventually went on to become supper themselves. We wound our way down, round and round, three twists of the staircase, before Paimon halted. I craned my neck around the bend to see what he could see.

Once upon a time this would have been a vast open space. Now it had been divided into three. To the right, through the glass of steamy windows I could see the kitchen. A few civilians were busy inside, chopping up what appeared to be a massive carcass. For the sake of my sanity, I assumed it was beef.

In front of us was a vestibule with a number of plain hardwood benches. Several shadow guards lounged here, a few dozing, the others chatting. They had their masks and leather gloves off, and now that I could see their faces they seemed a great deal less sinister than I'd supposed. They were young for the most part, pimply faced locals who needed to earn some cash.

To the left was the shadow guard base. It had been partitioned but there was no glass so you could view what was effectively a single large space containing a desk and some lockers, and a place where weapons were stored. There were several older chaps in there, poring over a map or something similar on the desk.

This presented a problem.

I pulled my head back and leaned down to Paimon. "You're going to have to throw that pillow as high as you can. Aim for the partition on the left. I'll do the rest."

He nodded his understanding.

I mentally rehearsed the moves and the words I would need and then grounding myself lifted my wand in front of my face.

"Go." The low command seemed to carry in the stairwell, but I didn't have time to worry about that.

Paimon scurried through to the vestibule and planted himself centrally.

"*What* is that?" someone shouted.

My turn to show myself.

I took a step, rounding the corner. In another few paces I was behind Paimon.

"*This* is a djinn," I told the astonished men, "and he's here to help you sleep."

"That's her!" One of the two guards nearest me on the benches stood as though to rush me. "The one we've spent all night looking for!"

The other remained where he was, looking more than a little scared, but their compatriots in the office made a move to join us.

"Now!" I told Paimon and he threw the pillow high into the air, twisting his wrist as he did so in order to make it spin. After that, everything happened in slow motion. Heads swivelled to watch the pillow rise and mouths opened as it began to fall.

I took aim with my wand, needing to get the timing just right. "*Pluma! Displodo.*" The pillow erupted and feathers flew everywhere, a white downy explosion that tickled and irritated as they began to float to the floor. As the shadow guards batted them away, I circled my wand gently, caressing the air around me. "*Somnus enim a dum.*" I kept my voice low, soothing, almost mournful.

As one, slowly and without harm, the guards slumped to the ground as the spell worked its magick and their bodies fell into a deep sleep. I prodded the nearest one with my boot. He emitted a pig-like snore. Perfection. Stepping carefully over him, I headed for the kitchen. Several of the workers had seen what had happened. Scared they would come at me with their carving knives or butcher's knives I raised my wand. I needn't have worried. These were ordinary citizens and they had no desire to pick a fight with a witch.

Only the old woman, sitting on a low stool by the fire and plucking a goose with a ferocity that Monsieur Emietter would have admired, appeared unphased. She smiled at me, a broad toothless grin, chuckling happily away to herself.

As I approached she threw the goose down at her feet and stood, holding her arms open.

"Welcome, welcome!" She laughed hard, like someone who hadn't done so in a very long time. "Me Codrina! Also witch!"

"I knew it," I said and wrapped her in a hug.

Retrieving Silvan from beneath the balcony was not at all plain sailing.

Codrina sent one of the chefs down to the nearby village to fetch help. He swiftly returned with a pair of strapping farm lads. The problem was, farm lads with huge muscles are not the best at abseiling castle walls. Nevertheless, we constructed a pulley system and I worked the sticky spell on them both so that they needn't fear falling from the ropes. Fortunately it only took one of them to carry Silvan and the other was then on hand to help haul the pair up, ably assisted by myself, Codrina, several of the chefs—who seemed particularly keen to get one over on the vampires—and Paimon of course.

Silvan hardly seemed to know me. His teeth chattered and he cried out in pain when we lay him on the stone flags of the balcony. I caressed his forehead. "You're going to be safe soon," I told him. "Really soon." I looked up at Codrina and she nodded.

"We take to village and hide," she told me. "I organise."

"Will they think to search there?" I asked, as

worried about the villagers' safety in the face of Grigor's wrath as much as my own and Silvan's.

"Not worry. Not worry." Codrina waved my concerns away and spoke rapidly in her own language. The two farm labourers lifted Silvan to carry him inside. "Careful!" she snapped at them. "Important cargo." She looked at me and winked.

I couldn't help but smile at her cheekiness in spite of my concerns. "Very important," I agreed.

While the chefs dismantled the harnesses and ropes we'd used I walked to the edge of the balcony and looked over. The Transylvanian landscape was bathed in sunshine, the snowy peaks of the Carpathians in the distance, sparkled.

Stunning.

But I couldn't wait to get away.

As I turned back for the door, a subdued electronic bong caught my attention. I frowned and glanced about me. The noise came again. This time I caught the direction of sound, and when I redoubled my search efforts, something shiny caught my attention. Tucked under one of the columns that held the mantle of the balustrade, lying on a bed of spongy moss and ivy... was my mobile phone. The screen had cracked but was otherwise in one piece.

I grabbed a hold of it hastily, imagining it slipping out of my grasp once more and falling to the forest floor below never to be seen again. The screen lit up as I touched it. Still no signal and only a slither of battery life left.

I glanced up at the castle walls looming large above me. The phone had fallen from the turrets above and not smashed into smithereens? The goddess had been looking out for me, after all.

"Well I'll be—"

I slipped inside the study and took a couple of photos of the large portrait hanging above the fire before my mobile died on me completely.

Time to see if I could charge it, find a signal and send these photos to Wizard Shadowmender.

CHAPTER SEVENTEEN

"I knew your great-grandmother." Codrina grinned toothlessly at me.

"You did?" That seemed unlikely to me. Gwyn had been dead for decades and I imagined Codrina was somewhere in her sixties. She had the appearance of a woman who had lived a hard life, working primarily with her hands, cooking and cleaning, and tending fires—with her magick of course. But then I hadn't known that Gwyn had visited Transylvania in the aftermath of the First World War, let alone any time more recently. "When?"

"Was a long time ago. She was kind to me. A good woman."

"She was," I agreed. "'Is' in some ways. Her ghost lives with me back at home."

Codrina laughed. She found everything hilarious. "She keeps grip on life even now? She still a fierce fighter."

We were sitting in the back of a large flatbed pick-up truck, with Silvan on a hastily constructed mattress of cushions and blankets at our feet. He slipped in and out of consciousness and seemed entirely unaware of his surroundings. When I reached to calm him, he felt hot to the touch.

I'd bid Paimon a fond farewell and sent him back to wherever djinns hang out when they are waiting to be summoned. It had been short and sweet, but he'd proven his worth. After she'd taken care of more of the guards with a sleeping draught she'd pre-prepared, Codrina had then hustled us to climb onto the back of a flatbed truck in the courtyard. Her organisational skills were formidable, almost as though she'd recognised what would be needed well in advance of my appearance in her kitchen. Once aboard, we'd hidden under a tarpaulin until the truck cleared the guards by the drawbridge. I counted the seconds until we were well away from the castle and the immediate danger seemed to fade. At some stage, five minutes into the journey, the truck stopped, and the driver rolled the tarpaulin back so that we could breathe a little easier.

The jeep turned off the main road and took back roads for another thirty minutes. The going was slower, the terrain more challenging, and we rocked about in the back. Silvan groaned from time to time and Codrina soothed him with words I didn't understand. The trees were dense and tall, and for the first time in days I breathed deeply and with relief. The forest was a friend to me, sheltering me in my time of need.

Finally we came to a tiny village—not much more than three houses and a few barns—and we slowed to a stop. A younger woman rushed out of one of the houses, wiping her hands on her apron, followed more slowly by two handsome and thick set young men. The woman spoke to Codrina in rapid fire Romanian. Codrina listened and nodded and turned to me.

"This is Irina, my daughter-in-law, and my sons Titus and Marius. They will look after your friend. I must return to the castle before the Master awakes."

"Do you have a phone?" I asked her. "I have to get in touch with Wizard Shadowmender back in the UK. He'll get us out of here." We'd left the castle in such a rush I hadn't even been able to go back to my room and grab my things.

"No phone." Codrina frowned.

"We have cell phone," Irina contradicted her mother-in-law.

"But no credit," Titus chipped in.

I regarded them with silent amazement. How had these people not progressed into the twenty-first century? "But you do have a charger, right?" I asked, crossing my fingers they had a modern mobile phone with a universal charger.

I'd been hoping for a place at some cheery hearth while I waited for my phone to charge—the charger did fit mine, thank the goddess—but actually we were taken down into a small basement room, cut underneath a much larger one, generally used to store root vegetables.

"What's this?" I shivered. There was no fire in here, and only a couple of oil lamps to give light. The walls ran with damp. Codrina's sons had brought Silvan down here while I plugged my phone in upstairs. He'd been placed on a bier in the centre of the room, which in itself was disconcerting, but at least he was off the cold ground.

Archibald's face twisted in slight disgust too, but he merely rolled his shoulders back in that kind of do-or-die way ex-members of the military have. No doubt he'd seen worse.

Irina regarded me solemnly with huge blue eyes. I guessed she was my age, but like her mother she lived a hard life here in the back of beyond. "For your safety," she told me. "It is unlikely you'll be out of here until tomorrow at the earliest. The Master's rage will know no bounds. His people will search everywhere for you. They will come here. You cannot be found. If you are, none of us will be spared."

I nodded and grimaced. That must not be allowed to happen. "Fair enough."

Titus clumped down the wooden stairs; his feet, clad in heavy work boots, were loud in the quiet room. He had an armful of blankets. Codrina followed him with a basket of supplies and a bucket of warm water. We set the supplies in the corner and then while Irina began to clean Silvan's wounds and splint his fingers, I followed the old witch back up the stairs.

"I am sorry to leave you this way, but I must not be absent from the castle for long."

"Thank you for all you have done." I hugged her. "I'm certain we wouldn't have made it without you."

Codrina smiled. "Witches always look after their own. Remember me to your great-grandmother."

"I definitely will," I promised, waving as she jumped back in the truck next to the man who had driven us to safety. I nodded my thanks at him and stood back. They ambled away, heading for the horror of Castle Iadului once more, the forest swallowing them up.

Back in the farmhouse I checked my phone impatiently. The battery had revived but only minutely. I unplugged it and carried it outside, wandering around the clearing until a quiet ting told me I had a signal.

What should I say? How could I convey the urgency of the situation?

I needed to send the photos I'd taken, but Wizard Shadowmender didn't have a phone or a computer. Rather, I'd have to send them to Penelope, or better still Ross Baines. I knew he'd recognise the urgency of the situation.

I scrolled through my contacts and found an email address I'd used for Ross previously, and quickly—channelling my inner Ethan Hunt once more—I typed, *Require extraction of two persons. In daylight. Triangulate position. URGENT.* I attached the best of the photos I had taken in the castle's study and pressed send. I hardly dared to breathe until the screen confirmed my message had been sent.

Then it died again.

I cast a glance at the milky sky above my head, as the trees danced around me, leaves scattering on the wind. *Send it home*, I begged. *Let them find us.*

Back in the basement Silvan appeared to be sleeping peacefully. The bruising and swelling of his face distorted his natural good looks and I feared touching him in case I hurt him.

Nonetheless I leaned over him and brushed his long floppy fringe away from his eyes, and gently soothed his head. "We'll be okay," I told him. "Wizard Shadowmender knows by now."

I sat back on a rickety old chair that Marius had brought down from the cottage above, every part of me ached or throbbed, and tears pricked at my eyes.

"He's a lucky man," Irina said, finishing up the bandaging of his left hand and laying it across his stomach. She smiled at me; her gentle face sympathetic to my plight.

"You think they could have killed him?" I asked, and my voice wobbled.

"Oh undoubtedly. It wouldn't be the first time." She turned and spat on the floor. "They're butchers up there. Pure evil. Capable of anything. I've seen it time and again. But no—" she nodded at me. "I meant he is lucky to have you. Codrina told me what you did. You're a superhero."

"What I did?" I repeated. I thought back over the past few days, particularly the last twenty-four hours. Talking to Ambassador Rubenscarfe. My 'trial', such as it was. Escaping my bedroom. Hanging onto a ledge for hours. Hiding in a small opening in the rockface below a balcony. Conjuring a djinn. Taking out a dozen shadow guards. Locating the source of magick at Castle Iadului.

It had been nothing really.

I started to shake. Those memories—of clinging to the castle walls by my fingertips while the virtually blind and badly-injured man I thought I might be in love with followed me on a thankless quest—would remain with me for an inordinately long time.

Irina wrapped a huge furry blanket around my shoulders and squeezed my shoulder. "There is soup in a flask here," she said, politely ignoring the tears streaming down my face. "You should take some sustenance and try and get some rest. Silvan will sleep. Dawn will bring good news, I'm certain."

The problem was we had the evening and the night to get through first.

Shortly before twilight I climbed up the steps for one last breath of fresh air and to visit the plumbed facilities. For the next ten or eleven hours I'd be making do with a potty. While Irina replenished the basket with more soup and fresh tea, along with half a loaf of freshly made bread and a chunk of hard cheese, I took the opportunity to head outside to find a signal once more and grab a quick look at my phone.

Just the one message. But it was from Ross!
Received. Hang tight.
Hang tight? I grimaced. If only he knew.
It was so like him to be concise though. I knew he'd be beavering away behind the scenes.

With the light failing fast I figured I should return to the basement. I trooped back inside, glad of the warmth of the fire, intending to put my mobile phone back on charge. Irina however had other ideas. She unclipped it and handed it back to me.

"I won't get a signal in the basement," I said.

She shook her head. "No. But you can't leave it here in case it is found."

"You think they'll actually come into the house?" I asked in alarm.

She nodded. "They don't care. They come here. Fly from the castle."

"As bats?"

"Yes. As bats. They land in the trees and slip down here and through any entry point they can find. They go where they like. No-one dares to challenge them."

"That's awful," I lamented. I couldn't live like that. "You should find a way to fight back."

Irina smiled, radiating a calm confidence. "We're not here to fight. Our families came here a long time ago. Our coven is spread throughout the forest that surrounds Castle Iadului. We keep an eye on what is happening and kerb their excesses. We help where we can and try to deter visitors. We're not in a position to launch a full out war on The Vampire Nation. I hope we never have to."

"That's not what the Ministry of Witches in the UK wants to happen," I agreed.

"Exactly. It would be costly and who knows how

we could contain the overspill into the mundane world."

"So you do what you can." I nodded in understanding, thinking of my father Erik Daemonne and his ongoing battle with The Mori.

"We do." Irina handed her basket over to me. "Go down into the basement. We will cover over the entrance to the sub-basement room. No matter what you hear, you must stay there all night. We will come for you in the morning."

"But—" I started to say.

Irina shook her head firmly. "No buts. Your young man can only remain safe as long as you do."

She had a point.

I nodded mutely, and tripped back down the stairs, intent on waiting out the night.

I slept on and off, slouching in my chair.

Time and again I would wake from troubled dreams, my heart beating loudly in my chest. Always Archibald—wakeful and watching—would give a little shake of his head. Still safe, that told me. We remained quiet, three little mice, scared of giving ourselves away.

I couldn't be sure what time it was, but during the early hours I woke with a start once more, catching my breath as I tried to run from something chasing me. This time Archibald but his finger to his mouth and pointed upstairs. I eased myself out of my chair and slid across the floor to join him, straining my ears to listen to the events unfolding somewhere above us.

Angry shouts. Curses, but not of the magickal kind. A couple of men bellowing. That would be Titus and Marius. The banging of doors. Breaking crockery. More shouting.

If Codrina and her family had been through this before it must cost them a fortune in broken household items.

Unless this time it was different.

Had Codrina been found out? Were her family suspected?

Worried that I'd put them in danger, I began to climb the ladder. Archibald hissed at me, but I waved him away.

A thump directly overhead froze me in my tracks. They were in the root cellar.

Behind me Silvan moaned. Not loudly, but my stomach churned in sudden panic. We couldn't be found. Silvan needed proper medical care. He was my responsibility.

The thump came again. As though someone was smacking the floor with a large heavy pole or something.

And again.

Hard enough that the ceiling shook, and dust and debris scattered to the floor. I darted a fearful look at the dark witch laid out on the bier behind me. I couldn't betray our hiding place to help Codrina's family. Instead, I scurried back down the ladder and across the floor and lay my hand on his forehead. "Hush," I murmured on an exhaled breath into his ear. "Not a sound, my love. Not a whisper."

He relaxed beneath my touch, and I lay my face next to his. Above us the vampires were rampaging. All we could do was hide out and wait.

At some stage around dawn, the hammering and shouting ceased. By then I'd slumped into an exhausted heap on the floor, but I jumped up with a start when the hatch was pulled open.

Titus poked his head through the gap and smiled at me, offering the thumbs up.

"You come," he said and, after quickly checking on Silvan I sped up the wooden steps, through the basement room above and on again to the cottage. Much as I'd imagined the furniture had been pulled about, items smashed, and every cupboard and potential hidey-hole searched.

I stood in the middle of the big downstairs room and turned about in dismay. The cottage had been wrecked.

Irina appeared tired, but the gleam of triumph in her eye told me all I needed to know. "They've gone," she told me.

"But the mess!" I commiserated.

She brushed that away. "Belongings mean nothing. Always there are new belongings. Everyone is safe. That's what matters.

"I'll help you clear up," I offered, bending to pick up the shards of a broken vase at my feet. It seemed the least I could do.

Irina reached out to take my arm. "No time," she said and pulled me towards the door. "Your ride is here."

I stepped outside, then almost collapsed in shock. A large blue range rover had been parked up in front of the cottage. The driver's door stood open and the driver himself, consulting a large ordnance survey, was in conversation with his navigator.

The navigator was none other than my great-grandmother, who obviously had some knowledge of the area. And the driver?

George.

Chapter Eighteen

After a whirlwind journey via range rover, private jet and then limousine (both of the latter loaned to Wizard Shadowmender by Sabien Laurent of all people) I arrived back at Whittle Inn just over fourteen hours later.

We'd stopped over briefly in London, where Silvan had been taken to a private hospital just off Celestial Street. I'd wanted to stay with him, but for a variety of reasons that hadn't been allowed. "You need to be debriefed," Penelope Quigwell had snipped at me. Debriefed I had been, for the next three hours.

But now, as the limousine wound its way down the motorway and along the back roads that led to Whittlecombe, Gwyn and Archibald had spent most of the journey catching up on their prior shared experiences in Transylvania, while Ross Baines tapped away at his laptop, his brow furrowed, his fingers moving at lightning speed. Everyone had ignored me for most of the journey.

George had driven all the way. At our final fuel stop at the motorway services, I'd grabbed a bathroom break and a steaming hot cup of coffee. Then before Penelope could protest, I'd slipped out of her grasp and plonked myself in the passenger seat. I put my feet up on the dash and glanced across at him. "So?" I asked. Even my voice sounded exhausted. "Would you care to explain?"

George shrugged tiredly. He had every right to look a little jaded given he'd been driving for hours both here and in Transylvania and through Romania, and like me had only had a few hours rest on the plane.

But ha! That faded in comparison to what I'd been through over the past few days.

"What can I tell you?" He told me now. "Wizard Shadowmender called me and asked for my assistance. He said you were in trouble. How could I turn him down?"

I smiled, touched that the detective still cared enough to come to my aid. "I'm grateful. Thank you."

"Don't any of you witches drive?" George asked.

"Couldn't they have sent someone else? I don't know why you have to rope me in." He didn't sound like he minded though, to be honest.

"I drive," I pointed out to him, although he knew that of course.

"Oh that's right. You drive. After a fashion."

I poked him in the ribs.

"Do you mind? I'm trying to concentrate here."

I snorted and took a sip of my coffee. It was still too hot and burned my mouth. I wafted at my mouth. "Ow."

"Serves you right," George muttered.

We drove in silence for a while, the hills rising and falling on either side of the road, the terrain becoming increasingly forested.

Nearly home.

"Will Silvan be okay?" George asked eventually.

"Of course!" I said this with huge confidence even though I had no real idea. Silvan had nine lives. Now we'd arrived back in the UK he would receive the medical treatment he needed; he would be fine. They'd assured me of that. But when would I hear from him again? Like Shadowmender, Silvan didn't carry a phone. He claimed to have no need of one.

"Good," George said.

I nursed my thoughts for a while. George

watched the road. Finally I couldn't stand it anymore. I had to tell him. I took a deep breath.

"George? About Silvan."

George took one hand off the steering wheel and held it up. He turned his head slightly and met my eyes. He looked a little sad. "It's fine." He shook his head.

"It's fine?"

How was it fine? How could George *know* it was fine? Now we were home would Silvan forget what we'd said to each other. Had either of us meant it? My feelings were a maelstrom, but according to George, Silvan and I were 'fine'.

"Yes." George turned his attention to the road once more.

He'd expected the news. How had he known about us? Was I the last to know?

It appeared so.

Whittle Inn was peculiarly silent.

Still devoid of guests, the inn had been shut up for nearly a week. Kat and Marc had been removed for their own safety. The rooms seemed unusually spacious without anyone in them although the ghosts had obviously remained in residence, most notably Florence. A fire burned in the grate in the bar at least, and a pile of baking books and a note pad and pens littered one of the dining tables. She'd clearly been working hard on her book in my absence.

Zephaniah appeared in front of me. "Welcome home, Miss Alf, and Mrs Daemonne." He nodded respectfully at Gwyn. She stood behind me, either inspecting the mantlepiece for dust, or admiring her portrait above the fire, one of the two. "Shall I collect your luggage?"

"I don't have any," I said. "I had to leave it all there."

"Such a goddess-forsaken castle, that one." Gwyn glowered. "You should be glad you abandoned everything, my dear. In fact anything you did bring back with you will need burning."

I looked down at the robes I'd been wearing for what felt like days. It probably wasn't a bad idea. I plucked my wand from one pocket and my mobile phone with its cracked screen from another and set them on the bar.

"I could really do with a hot chocolate or something, Zephaniah. Is Florence around? Or Monsieur Emietter?"

"Florence is seeing to the bedrooms, Miss," Zephaniah replied. I frowned. Whose bedrooms?

"Never mind hot chocolate. You look like you're in need of a stiff drink," Gwyn said.

"I think we could all do with one," Penelope said. She and Ross were setting up their laptops on a spare table. It looked like they were settling in for the immediate future.

"Are you staying?" I asked.

"Yes." Penelope peered over the top of her spectacles at me. "Is that a problem?"

I withered in her glare. "No. Of course not."

I turned to George, expecting him to say goodbye. "Make mine a whisky," he said.

"You're staying too?" I asked in confusion.

"Wizard Shadowmender asked me to. Just for a few days."

"He did?"

George nodded and I looked about at the clan gathered around me. Why had Wizard Shadowmender wanted everyone here?

I couldn't figure it out and a sudden wave of giddiness put paid to me actually trying. Exhausted I waved at everyone present and turned for the stairs.

"I'm going to bed," I said.

I drifted upwards on a downy cushion of heavenly comfort, floating on a warm breeze. I thought the sun was shining, but the pitter patter of soft raindrops suggested otherwise. I didn't want to wake up. I'd be happy staying right there where I was, safe and warm.

Mr Hoo had other ideas, for it was he who pitter-pattered around the top of my duvet cover, peering down at me hopefully. When I finally opened my eyes and blinked up at him he twitted a welcome.

"Of course I'm alive," I mumbled, and tried to return to that sanctuary of sleep I'd been forced to forsake.

"Hooooo. Hooooooooo."

"No it isn't," I said. He'd just told me it was nearly midday. That would mean I'd been asleep for ten hours. "It can't be." I reached for the little alarm clock on my nightstand and blinked at the numbers until I could focus on them. My little owl friend had not been making it up.

I huffed sadly. "I'd better get up then." Not least to find out why I had an inn full of people, none of whom were paying guests.

I took a bath. Not one of my long luxurious

bubble baths, but a rather functional-dip-with-added-hair-wash. I certainly felt better afterwards, a little more awake, and in need of some serious sustenance. Hoping I'd be able to drag Florence away from her books so she could drum me up a hearty late breakfast I headed downstairs.

I can't say I was entirely surprised to find that Wizard Shadowmender had arrived from Surbiton and Mr Kephisto from nearby Abbotts Cromleigh. Unfortunately, it looked as though breakfast would have to remain on hold.

"What's going on?" I asked as soon as greetings had been exchanged.

"Well, Penelope, with the able assistance of young Ross here, have been digging around and they've found a little intelligence that you might find interesting."

"That's good news," I said, thinking longingly of scrambled egg on hot toast with lashings of fresh butter and a good sprinkle of pepper.

"We want to nip The Vampire Nation's attack on you—and on witches in general—in the bud. Once and for all."

"Yes. That *would* be good." I wondered how many mugs of tea I could drown in five minutes and would it be standard Yorkshire Tea or English Breakfast?

"And we also have a plan," Wizard Shadowmender confided.

"Ah," I said, pleased I no longer had to strive to be the adult in the room. "Thank goodness someone has one of those."

A little after midnight the bats returned to Whittle Inn.

I'd been sitting alone on the front step for an hour or so, wrapped in a large old cardigan that Millicent had once given me, a scarf around my neck and nursing a dark rum and coke. I'd hated to do it, but I'd locked Mr Hoo inside my bedroom. I hadn't wanted him on the loose.

I pretended not to notice the bats arriving, and to be sure they had done so quietly and without fuss. However, every one of my senses, every nerve and fibre had strained to feel for them. Inwardly I shuddered with revulsion, remembering the feeling of Grigor's repulsive dry hands around my neck and the way his elongated yellow claw of a thumbnail had penetrated the delicate skin at my throat.

No doubt he was up there in one of the huge oak trees at the end of the drive, right now, watching me as I drained the last of my drink. I stood and stretched out my back and neck and stiffly turned to walk inside, heading for my cheerful fire and perhaps a refill.

Silly me. I had neglected to close the front door properly.

I walked to the fire, the only light in the room, keeping my back to the door, and placed my glass on the mantelpiece. Before I could turn back I heard the flip flap of tiny wings, and a blast of icy air heralded the arrival of the vampires.

Grigor.

I had known he would come, but I still found his presence in my beloved inn unnerving. The old vampire stood in the middle of the lounge bar area, flanked on each side by half a dozen of his kind, for the most part young and beautiful. Neither Sabien nor Melchior were among them, but there was one there I did recognise, and my gaze lingered on him.

"Alfhild." The familiar reptilian tongue slithered a greeting. The drooling of a man centuries old. One who now struggled to hunt and to feed to find the nutrients he needed to revitalise his appearance.

"Prince Grigor." I nodded, pouring ice into my expression.

"Your arrogance is your undoing, my child. Did you imagine I wouldn't follow you here? We have business that remains unfinished."

"Your trial was a complete sham." I finally found my voice. "It was meaningless. You can't touch me here."

"I passed sentence."

I lifted my chin. "Your sentence will not stand here. I have friends in high places, and you should not dare to touch me."

Grigor made a tsk-ing sound. "Such defiance. Justice must be served. You were found guilty."

I shook my head. "You should leave while the going is good, Prince Grigor."

He cackled, a screeching high-pitched breathless hilarity that reminded me of nails on a chalkboard. "Not until I have done what I came here to do. And it is truly fitting that it should happen here where my son met his unnatural end. You cannot escape, Alfhild. Judgement was passed and the sentence must be carried out on the one who murdered my son—"

"I didn't kill Thaddeus."

"That sentence was death!" He snarled like a

wild bear. I'd forgotten how fast he could move, but suddenly he was on me. Maybe I'd imagined I was ready for the onslaught that I knew would come my way, but he moved so quickly, and he was so strong, that he still took me completely by surprise. I buckled under the weight of him as he forced me to my knees, yanking my hair back hard so that my throat was exposed.

A glint of bright white fang and the flashing of the blackest of eyes, and then we were both bowled over. I sprawled on the floor coughing and hacking, beating at the air, dangerously close to the grate where the fire burned. Grigor's cloak of blue wafted over my head as he jumped to his feet and reacted to whatever had knocked us over.

"*Quiescat*." The command floated serenely out of the air and everything stopped at once. "Lights," the voice ordered. Instantly the bar was flooded with illumination as every light and lamp in the room was switched on, every candle burst into flame. The vampires stood stock still, eyes twitching nervily as they surveyed the legion of witches surrounding them, wands drawn and faces grim.

Gwyn, Penelope, Mr Kephisto, Finbarr, Mara and Millicent, along with a dozen others we had invited from around the region who had heeded our urgent clarion call. They all stood to attention, focused entirely on the threat in front of us. Wizard Shadowmender stepped out of their ranks and gently aimed his wand at Prince Grigor who'd been caught red-handed when the lights went on, kneeling over George.

George had been the missile that had knocked us both to the ground. Now pale, he'd been pinned to the floor. Grigor's leathery hand was wrapped around the detective's smooth neck.

"If you would be so good as to unhand DS Gilchrist, I would be much obliged," Wizard Shadowmender said, his wand emitting tiny sparks, a warning of what might occur if Grigor refused.

"What is the meaning of this?" Grigor hissed. "You can't come at me mob-handed. I'm a diplomat."

Shadowmender flicked his wand. Electricity buzzed through the air between him and the elderly vampire. Grigor released his hold of George and stood. One of the younger vampires moved against the wizard, covering the ground between them in a nanosecond.

But Penelope was faster. "*Lignumatus!*"

The young male vampire shrieked and fell to the floor with a heavy thud, his limbs stiff, his face in rictus.

Grigor halted mid-step, glancing down at his young protégé in horror. "You will pay for that," he snarled at Penelope.

"Come, come now, Grigor," Wizard Shadowmender urged him as though they were merely embarking on a game of Tiddlywinks. "All these threats of retribution. They won't get you anywhere."

"The Vampire Nation seek justice for the loss of my son. The Vampire Nation—"

"Have no further interest in your case against young Alfhild here. They have dropped all charges and have disavowed your *Vampiri* clan as a credible part of their organisation."

Grigor's pale face turned sour. "They have no right to—" he thundered, but Wizard Shadowmender held up his hand.

"They have every right, Grigor, as you well know." He looked over at me. "Are you alright, Alfhild?"

I nodded, a little shaken, but pleased to see George climbing to his feet too. I rolled away from the fire and reached for George. Taking his arm, I led him out of harm's way.

"Murderess," Grigor hissed after me.

"You are much mistaken Grigor, and it makes

you appear weak and foolish." Wizard Shadowmender pointed at the other vampires in the room. "One of your young hanger's-on knows the truth."

Grigor looked around uncertainly. "But I already established motive," he said. "Alfhild Daemonne hates vampires just as her great-grandmother before her did."

"Your hatred of her great-grandmother blinded you to the truth. You merely established a possible motive for one suspect. You haven't considered any others." Wizard Shadowmender's wand picked out one handsome young man in particular. "Including one of your other sons."

The young man in question stepped forward with menace. "Don't listen to them, Father."

"Absurd." Grigor waved the suggestion away.

"Isn't it the case that this young man, Gorka Corinthian I believe, stayed here with Thaddeus when they both attended the wedding last October?"

"Yes, I was here for the wedding. I was supporting my friend Melchior," Gorka said, but the elderly Wizard ignored him, addressing the old prince once more.

"And isn't it true that none of your sons have ever really seen eye-to-eye? That there's always been a great deal of rivalry for both your limited affection and your substantial wealth?"

Gorka interjected again, "Ignore this nonsense, Father."

"And since the disappearance of your oldest son, wouldn't it be fair to suggest that your remaining sons, Thaddeus and Gorka became even more combative?"

Grigor regarded Gorka for the first time. "My number three son always had a rivalry with his older brothers. But he would never kill Thaddeus—"

Wizard Shadowmender shrugged. "There's only one castle to inherit. Thaddeus was successful in his own right, but Gorka has always had to rely on others to support his lifestyle."

I was impressed. Penelope and Ross had done their homework. They'd briefed the wizard on all of Gorka's various business failures and property development fiascos.

"Perhaps Gorka wanted a larger slice of the pie?" Wizard Shadowmender suggested.

Penelope nodded. "We have no evidence, but we believe that Gorka may have had something to do with the mysterious disappearance of your oldest son too. Naturally we will leave that to *Vampiri* to investigate in the future." Having said her piece, she bowed and stepped back into the circle of witches.

Grigor frowned.

Wizard Shadowmender pressed home his point. "Whoever tied Thaddeus to that chair needed superhuman strength. I'm not sure Alfhild could have managed that on her own. It seems more likely that one of his own kind was able to overcome your son. They tied him to the chair and positioned him very precisely. They then sabotaged the lights in this room, knowing full well that in the morning, someone would open the curtains and Thaddeus would be dead before anybody could react."

"Father—" Gorka wheedled.

"Silence!" Grigor roared, the pain in his voice unmistakeable. "I need to think."

Wizard Shadowmender nodded at Penelope who stepped forward with a wad of printouts. "We took it upon ourselves to discuss our findings with our opposite numbers in The Vampire Nation. They have had Gorka under surveillance for some time regarding his dubious undertakings, including—and of most interest to us—selling off Thaddeus's Paris house and impersonating his brother in business dealings."

"Father?" Gorka tried once more. "I can explain."

"Will you shut up!" Grigor trumpeted.

Penelope held up another sheet of paper. "Gorka and his brother had a little spat on the evening before Thaddeus was killed. There were numerous witnesses to this including Sabien Laurent and his son Melchior. Both of them have offered to testify in open court to the truth of this statement."

Wizard Shadowmender nodded. "Indeed, Melchior himself has admitted that on numerous occasions, Gorka spoke of stepping into his brother's shoes, of finding some way to inveigle his way to the top of the tree, ready to take your place when the sun rises for the final time on your dark reign in Transylvania. As it will."

Grigor seemed to crumple into himself. He stood in the middle of a circle of witches, all with their wands trained on him, and realised the game had ended. Whether he believed I was innocent or not, it was clear that his son had betrayed him in a variety of ways.

When he spoke again, his voice was so quiet I had to strain to hear him. His bitterness was apparent. "I would rather my kingdom was handed over to a pox-ridden peasant than my treacherous son."

"But Father—" Gorka reached for the prince. Grigor's rage could no longer be contained. He lashed out with his right arm, catching Gorka under the chin and knocking him backwards. He tumbled into the waiting arms of the other vampires.

Gorka flailed, grabbing at cloaks, fighting to remain upright.

"Please!" he begged.

Grigor flung his arms up in fury and the inn seemed to rock with the force of his sudden fury. "Traitor! he screamed. "Destroy him!" As one, we witches raced forward to stop the butchery, but Gorka's terrified shrieks rent through the dark night for only a moment and were then abruptly silenced as the vampires fell upon him, tearing him to shreds.

EPILOGUE

"You've been polishing that spot for ten minutes."

I looked up to see Charity staring at me quizzically. I dropped my duster, but quickly grabbed it again and moved a foot to my right. The wood of the bar shone in the firelight. The mirrors sparkled so brightly they almost dazzled. She was right. My mind was elsewhere.

"I thought you'd appreciate a cuppa." She sidled over to me to place a mug of tea in front of me. "When are you planning to reopen the inn?"

It had been well over a week since the vampires had disappeared back to Transylvania. Ambassador Rubenscarfe had been recalled to London but had yet to return from Transylvania. Wizard Shadowmender had received an official apology from his counterpart in The Vampire Nation who had also reprimanded the Transylvanian *Vampiri*. Everyone had begun to return to normal.

Everyone except me, that is.

I couldn't shake the fear that had gripped me from the moment Sabien had turned up on my doorstep.

Every time I closed my eyes at night I could hear Gorka's final scream. My dreams were full of images of sheer drops and narrow ledges. I'd wake sweating and shaking and then be scared to try for sleep once more. I'd lost weight because I couldn't eat. I had bags under my eyes. I felt hyper all of the time and I just needed to be busy. Busy, busy, busy. Every part of the inn had been cleaned and polished. I'd even tried my hand at redecorating parts of it, and as everyone knows, I'm really not that good at such things.

The Ghostly Clean-Up Crew, who would have happily redecorated the whole inn had I asked them to, were never summonsed. I wanted to be alone, unharried, but within ear shot of the normal sounds of the inn such as Zephaniah's gramophone, Mr Hoo's hunting calls and contented twittering, the washing machine on its endless cycles, Monsieur Emietter's tuneless singing in the kitchen, the banging of the old boiler in the back room, or even the Devonshire Fellows rehearsing in the attic.

My friends had tried to re-engage me with the normality of my wonky life. Finbarr. Millicent. Charity. Gwyn—they all tried and failed. Florence, in desperation, had downed tools on her book, attempting to gee me up with all my favourite cakes, but even coffee and pecan had failed to kickstart my appetite.

Charity had called George, and he—bless his heart—had driven over from Exeter and tried to talk to me, but I kept them both at arm's length. They were such special friends, but I found I couldn't relate to them and didn't want to share all I'd been through. Was this how Gwyn had felt? Is this why she never spoke about her time at Castle Iadului?

I could finally understand her absolute loathing of vampires now.

The one time I tried to broach the subject with her I choked at the last moment, unable to articulate my thoughts. She'd regarded me through troubled eyes, a sympathetic half-smile playing at the corner of her mouth, then nodded once and turned away.

We left it at that.

It made me sad.

I haunted the corridors, straightening pictures,

dusting the skirting boards, chasing giant house spiders into dark corners or under the floorboards, but feeling disengaged and remembering how in those long terrible moments at the castle I had longed for Whittle Inn. Now that I was home, why couldn't it soothe my troubled soul?

I pretended I didn't see the concerned looks or hear the hushed murmurings. Millicent suggested I had some kind of post-traumatic-stress disorder, but I dismissed this—unkindly—as just another of her ridiculous ramblings.

So now I tried to force myself into the present. Charity was right. I should reopen the inn. It would give me something besides myself to focus on.

"Let's make some phone calls," I said. "Tell everyone we'll reopen."

But Charity had gone, and the mug of tea in front of me was stone cold. I'd been staring into space for ages.

Someone drifted past the window to my right. Ned. Pushing his wheelbarrow around the side. The light was poor, thanks to the low clouds and thick sea mist that had drifted inland. It would be growing dark soon.

Speckled Wood called to me and for the first time since I'd returned home, and despite my stupor,

I heard it. It would be good to get outside and taste the salt in the mist and breathe deeply of the chilly air. I chucked my duster under the bar, grabbed my outside robe and a scarf, and bundled up.

Mr Hoo soared overhead as I tramped along the path to the wood. The canopy rose suddenly out of the mist, the deciduous trees' branches appearing increasingly spindly. One good storm and all the leaves would fall for the year.

Depending on the way the wind blew, that would keep Ned busy in the grounds for months.

I trailed my fingers along the trunks of the trees I passed, stopping occasionally to press my ear to the thick damp moss that grew up some of the trunks, listening to the heart of the forest. Strong sturdy beats. Healthy sounds. We'd come a long way since the marsh malaise in the early part of the summer.

Normally a stroll through the forest would lift my spirits with every step, but today I felt lost and disconnected. Maybe—the goddess forbid—it would always be this way now. Perhaps no-one would ever understand what I'd been through. Except Grandmama.

Or Silvan...

As I approached the clearing in the centre of Speckled Wood, I imagined I was seeing things. A tall figure, clad head to toe in black. Black boots and trousers, black cloak pulled up over his head. Black hair, dark, dark eyes. But not the dead black eyes of a vampire. Far from it. These eyes sparkled with life and laughter, despite the now yellowing bruising around both them and his cheekbones, and the stitches across the bridge of his nose.

He tried not to smile when he saw me, but he couldn't help himself.

My heart lurched at the sight of him. I tried to rush towards him, but the strength ebbed from my knees. I slipped towards the ground and suddenly he was there, kneeling with me, his strong arms around me, pulling me to him.

"I think you've fallen for me, Alfhild," he whispered into my hair, always ready with a joke, making fun of my sudden weakness, this one a combination of sleep deprivation, lack of sustenance and too much emotion. I tried to laugh, I really did, but instead I burst into tears. I pressed my face into his robes to stifle my howling anguish. Nevertheless the whole forest bore witness. He rocked me gently, stroking my back and smoothing my hair, allowing me the space to shake and sob.

"What is it?" he asked eventually, when most of

the tempest seemed to have passed. "Can you tell me?"

I shook my head, sniffing hard. "It's just... I... was so SCARED!"

Silvan squeezed me tighter. "Of course you were. Any sensible person would have been."

"I could have got us killed," I wailed.

"But you didn't." Silvan's voice was calm and quiet, and low in my ear. "You looked at the situation. You found a solution. You might have left me there, but you didn't. You were scared but you saw what needed doing and you did it anyway."

"I was weak," I sniffled.

"No." We swayed together as he added, "You're the bravest person I know. You're a fantastic witch and a wonderful woman."

He drew away and held me at arms' length, forcing me to look at him. "You're *my* woman. The only one I want to be with."

My bottom lip quivered, tears still spilling down my cheeks.

There was no hint of mischief now, and no doubting the sincerity in his eyes. "I love you, Alfie."

He'd said it before, and I'd imagined it had been meaningless because it was a statement made in a moment of extreme duress. Now my sobs stuck in my throat. "I l.. l.. love you too," I stuttered.

His head ducked towards mine, his gaze briefly raking my soul. "Of course you do," he laughed softly and then his warm lips met mine and I cleaved to him as though I had been waiting for him my whole life.

The wind blew around us, scattering leaves from the trees like so much natural confetti, while the fear inside me dissipated like mist on a warm spring morning.

PLEASE CONSIDER LEAVING A REVIEW?

If you have enjoyed reading *The Great Witchy Cake Off*, please consider leaving me a review.

Reviews help to spread the word about my writing, which takes me a step closer to my dream of writing full time.

If you are kind enough to leave a review, you could also consider joining my Author Street Team on Facebook – Jeannie Wycherley's Fiendish Street Team. As it is a closed group you will need to let me know you left a review when you apply.

You can find my fiendish team at

PLEASE CONSIDER LEAVING A REVIEW?

www.facebook.com/ groups/JeannieWycherleysFiends

You'll have the chance to Beta read and get your hands-on advanced review eBook copies from time to time. I also appreciate your input when I need some help with covers, blurbs etc. We have a giggle.

Or sign up for my newsletter eepurl.com/cN3Q6L to keep up to date with what I'm doing next!

WONKY CONTINUES

Witching in a Winter Wonkyland: A Wonky Inn Christmas Cozy Mystery

Coughs and sneezes spread diseases!

It's the most wonderful time of the year.

Unless you're Alfhild Daemonne that is.

This year she's been so looking forward to the Yule time festivities, but wouldn't you know it, the wattle-and-daub walls of her ancient wonky inn are ringing to the sound, not of sleigh bells, but of sick ghosts.

Who knew ghosts could catch the flu?

And let's not forget there's been a murder in Whittle Forest. Some of the locals are convinced there's a demonic Beast on the loose, and naturally they're pointing the finger at Alf and her guests.

Factor in a homeless reindeer, a grumpy faery

who detests Christmas, along with Alf missing her beau, and there's plenty here for lovers of Christmas murder novels with added humour.

Witching in a Winter Wonkyland is a standalone Christmas cozy mystery that complements the Wonky Inn series as a whole.

You'll love this crazy cast of witches, wizards, faeries, ghosts and pantomime villains.

And not forgetting Mr Hoo of course.

This new Wonky Inn Christmas mystery is best served with a glass of your favourite tipple and a heart full of love.

THE WONKY STORY BEGINS...

The Wonkiest Witch: Wonky Inn Book 1

Alfhild Daemonne has inherited an inn.

And a dead body.

Estranged from her witch mother, and having committed to little in her thirty years, Alf surprises herself when she decides to start a new life.

She heads deep into the English countryside intent on making a success of the once popular inn. However, discovering the murder throws her a curve ball. Especially when she suspects dark magick.

Additionally, a less than warm welcome from several locals, persuades her that a variety of folk – of both

THE WONKY STORY BEGINS…

the mortal and magickal persuasions – have it in for her.

The dilapidated inn presents a huge challenge for Alf. Uncertain who to trust, she considers calling time on the venture.

Should she pack her bags and head back to London?

Don't be daft.

Alf's magickal powers may be as wonky as the inn, but she's dead set on finding the murderer.

Once a witch always a witch, and this one is fighting back.

A clean and cozy witch mystery.

Take the opportunity to immerse yourself in this fantastic new witch mystery series, from the author of the award-winning novel, **Crone**.

Grab Book 1 of the Wonky Inn series, ***The Wonkiest Witch,*** on Amazon now.

The Wonky Inn Series

The Wonkiest Witch: Wonky Inn Book 1
The Ghosts of Wonky Inn: Wonky Inn Book 2
Weird Wedding at Wonky Inn: Wonky Inn Book 3
Fearful Fortunes and Terrible Tarot: Wonky Inn Book 4
The Mystery of the Marsh Malaise: Wonky Inn Book 5
The Mysterious Mr Wylie: Wonky Inn Book 6
The Great Witchy Cake Off: Wonky Inn Book 7
The Witch Who Killed Christmas: Wonky Inn Christmas Special

More Wonky Wonderfulness Coming Soon

Vengeful Vampire at Wonky Inn: Wonky Inn Book 8

… THE WONKY INN SERIES

Witching in a Winter Wonklyland: Wonky Inn Christmas Special

Also By

Midnight Garden: The Extra Ordinary World Novella Series Book 1

Beyond the Veil

Crone

A Concerto for the Dead and Dying

Deadly Encounters: A collection of short stories

Keepers of the Flame: A love story

Non-Fiction

Losing my best Friend: Thoughtful support for those affected by dog bereavement or pet loss

Follow Jeannie Wycherley

Find out more at on the website www.jeanniewycherley.co.uk

You can tweet Jeannie

twitter.com/Thecushionlady

Or visit her on Facebook for her fiction www.facebook.com/jeanniewycherley

Sign up for Jeannie's newsletter

eepurl.com/cN3Q6L

More Dark Fantasy from Jeannie Wycherley

Crone

A twisted tale of murder, magic and salvation.

Heather Keynes' teenage son died in a tragic car accident.

Or so she thinks.

However, deep in the countryside, an ancient evil has awoken ... intent on hunting local residents.

No-one is safe.

When Heather takes a closer look at a series of coincidental deaths, she is drawn reluctantly into the company of an odd group of elderly Guardians. Who are they, and what is their connection to the Great Oak?

Why do they believe only Heather can put an end to centuries of horror?

Most important of all, who is the mysterious old woman in the forest and what is it that feeds her anger?

When Heather determines the true cause of her son's death, she is hell-bent on vengeance. Determined to halt the march of the Crone once and for all, hatred becomes Heather's ultimate weapon and furies collide to devastating effect.

Crone – winner of a *Chill with a Book Readers' Award* (February 2018) and an *Indie B.R.A.G Medallion* (November 2017).

Praise for *Crone*

'A real page turner, hard to put down.'

'Stunningly atmospheric! Gothic & timeless set in the beautifully described Devon landscape …. Twists and turns, nothing predictable or disappointing.'

– Amazon reviewer

'Atmospheric, enthralling story-telling, and engaging characters'

– Amazon Reviewer

'Full of creepy, witchy goodness'

– The Grim Reader

'Wycherley has a talent for storytelling and a penchant for the macabre'

– Jaci Miller

Beyond the Veil

Upset the dead at your peril… Because the keepers of souls are not particularly forgiving.

Death is not the end. Although Detective Adam Chapple has always assumed it is.

When his ex-wife is killed, the boundaries between life and death, fantasy and reality, and truth and lies begin to dissolve. Adam's main suspect for the murder, insists that she's actually his star witness.

She claims she met the killer once before.

When she died.

As part of his investigation, Adam seeks out the help of self-proclaimed witch, Cassia Veysie who insists she can communicate with the dead. However, the situation rapidly deteriorates when a bungled séance rips open a gateway to a sinister world beyond the veil, and unquiet spirits are unleashed into the world.

Can Cassia and Adam find a way to shore up the breach in the veil and keep the demons at bay?

With time running out and a murderer on the loose, the nightmare is only just beginning ...

Praise for Beyond the Veil

'A 5-star winner from Queen of the Night Terrors'

– Amazon reviewer.

'Really got my heart pounding'

– Amazon reviewer.

'A nerve racking, nail-biting, spine tingling, sweat producing, thrilling storyline that keeps you on a razor's edge the entire tale'

– ARC reviewer.

'Female Stephen King!'

– Amazon reviewer.

MORE DARK FANTASY FROM JEANNIE WYCHERLEY

Crone

A twisted tale of murder, magic and salvation.

Heather Keynes' teenage son died in a tragic car accident.

Or so she thinks.

However, deep in the countryside, an ancient evil has awoken ... intent on hunting local residents.

No-one is safe.

When Heather takes a closer look at a series of coincidental deaths, she is drawn reluctantly into the company of an odd group of elderly Guardians. Who are they, and what is their connection to the Great Oak?

Why do they believe only Heather can put an end to centuries of horror?

Most important of all, who is the mysterious old woman in the forest and what is it that feeds her anger?

When Heather determines the true cause of her son's death, she is hell-bent on vengeance. Determined to halt the march of the Crone once and for all, hatred becomes Heather's ultimate weapon and furies collide to devastating effect.

Crone – winner of a *Chill with a Book Readers' Award* (February 2018) and an *Indie B.R.A.G Medallion* (November 2017).

Praise for *Crone*

'A real page turner, hard to put down.'

'Stunningly atmospheric! Gothic & timeless set in the beautifully described Devon landscape .... Twists and turns, nothing predictable or disappointing.' – Amazon reviewer

'Atmospheric, enthralling story-telling, and engaging characters' – Amazon Reviewer

'Full of creepy, witchy goodness' – The Grim Reader

MORE DARK FANTASY FROM JEANNIE WYCHERLEY

'Wycherley has a talent for storytelling and a penchant for the macabre' – Jaci Miller

Beyond the Veil

Upset the dead at your peril... Because the keepers of souls are not particularly forgiving.

Death is not the end. Although Detective Adam Chapple has always assumed it is.

When his ex-wife is killed, the boundaries between life and death, fantasy and reality, and truth and lies begin to dissolve. Adam's main suspect for the murder, insists that she's actually his star witness.

She claims she met the killer once before.

When she died.

As part of his investigation, Adam seeks out the help of self-proclaimed witch, Cassia Veysie who insists she can communicate with the dead. However, the situation rapidly deteriorates when a bungled séance rips open a gateway to a sinister world beyond the veil, and unquiet spirits are unleashed into the world.

Can Cassia and Adam find a way to shore up the breach in the veil and keep the demons at bay?

With time running out and a murderer on the loose, the nightmare is only just beginning …

Praise for Beyond the Veil

'A 5-star winner from Queen of the Night Terrors' – Amazon reviewer.

'Really got my heart pounding' – Amazon reviewer.

'A nerve racking, nail-biting, spine tingling, sweat producing, thrilling storyline that keeps you on a razor's edge the entire tale' – ARC reviewer.

'Female Stephen King!' – Amazon reviewer.

COMING SOON

The Municipality of Lost Souls by Jeannie Wycherley

Described as a cross between Daphne Du Maurier's *Jamaica Inn*, and TV's *The Walking Dead*, but with ghosts instead of zombies, *The Municipality of Lost Souls* tells the story of Amelia Fliss and her cousin Agatha Wick.

In the otherwise quiet municipality of Durscombe, the inhabitants of the small seaside town harbour a deadly secret.

Amelia Fliss, wife of a wealthy merchant, is the lone voice who speaks out against the deadly practice of the wrecking and plundering of ships on the rocks in Lyme bay, but no-one appears to be listening to her.

COMING SOON

As evil and malcontent spread like cholera throughout the community, and the locals point fingers and vow to take vengeance against outsiders, the dead take it upon themselves to end a barbaric tradition the living seem to lack the will to stop.

Set in Devon in the UK during the 1860s, *The Municipality of Lost Souls* is a Victorian Gothic ghost story, with characters who will leave their mark on you forever.

If you have previously enjoyed *Crone* or *Beyond the Veil*, you really don't want to miss this novel.

Sign up for my newsletter or join my Facebook group today.

Printed in Great Britain
by Amazon